HOW TO CATCH A VET

SPECIAL EDITION

CHESTER FALLS
BOOK SIX

ANA ASHLEY

Illustrated by
COVERS BY JULES

DEDICATION

To everyone who can't see their own beauty and worth.
Trust me.
You're seen.

Ana

ABOUT HOW TO CATCH A VET

The first thing I learned at Vet school was to always expect the unexpected.
Well, I sure never saw Santiago Torres or his adorable Great Dane coming.

Santi is everything I'm not. Tall, confident, overbearing, and if I'm to believe his advances, he's also very experienced in...well, you know what.
I always play safe, but it's time to ditch the v-card. We couldn't be more different, but that doesn't matter because this is just a one time thing.

I'm not going to want more, right?
I'm not going to fall for him, right?

How to Catch a Vet is the sixth book in the Chester Falls series and features an opposites attract story between a virgin and a player, a Great Dane with a tendency to rescue- read kidnap- other people's pets, and a small town like no other.

"Hey, Dad. Hey, Mom," I said into the screen.

"Happy anniversary, sweetie," they both sang.

God, I missed my parents. Only they would celebrate the one-year anniversary of the opening of my vet practice. Because it's a milestone, and they love a celebration.

"Thanks. How are you doing? I see the weather is great out there, as always."

I saw the pool and the clear blue sky behind them, and I was only ten percent jealous because summer had arrived in Chester Falls, but sadly, I had no pool.

"We're wonderful, sweetie. You could have this too. We told you to sell the house and open up here. You'd be closer to us."

"I know, Mom, but Florida is *your* dream, and I've always loved it here. I'm happy being back home. Reopening Grandpa's practice is a dream come true. I have so many plans for this place."

They looked at each other, and I knew they would love to have me there but were also happy with my decision.

"He'd be very proud of you, Micah," my dad said.

"Thanks, Dad. I think so too."

"Doctor Sawyer, your next patient is here," my assistant called from the door.

"Thanks, April. Send them in, please," I said.

I closed down the tab on my computer where, before my parents called, I'd been drafting the third email to the construction company that I'd hired to build my animal sanctuary.

"Mom, Dad, I have to go. I'll speak to you soon, okay? Love you."

There was a knock on the door, followed by one of my favorite four-legged patients and her dad.

"Micah, I was telling April how I think you need a little bit of color in your reception area. Maybe some pictures of pets on the walls and sparkle. You definitely need some sparkle. I read about this paint you can use that has glitter in it—it's very safe and nontoxic—and it would be perfect for one of the walls. The animals would love it. I bet they'd be less scared of coming to the doctor if they were distracted by something pretty. I mean, April is lovely, but you know, she doesn't quite...sparkle."

I bit the inside of my cheek to stop myself from laughing aloud.

"Hi, Tom, how are you doing?" I asked, taking the kitten carrier from him and placing it on the examination table.

He let out a big sigh. "Oh, you know. I always get a little nervous when I bring her in."

"There's no need. You take really good care of her. I'm sure there's nothing to worry about. Unless you've noticed any change in her behavior pattern, sleep, or eating?"

It was normal for the owners to be more nervous

around vets than their pets, so I liked to reassure them. But there was always the possibility that pets could develop a condition or illness that could go undetected until they came for the annual check.

"No, she's the same old queen of the castle and owner of my heart," he said, looking at Coco adoringly.

"And what does Wren think about that?" I said, raising a brow.

"Oh, he knows," Tom said, waving it off. "There's plenty of love in my rainbow heart for my little girl and my big man."

I laughed. Tom's fiancé, Wren, went to my high school, and even though we were in different years, I remembered the popular football player who I'd admired from afar. Tall, with a broad back and muscles for days, physically, he was totally my type. He'd been one of the reasons I'd realized I was into guys rather than girls, even though he wasn't out then.

I opened the door to the carrier, and Coco came out, going straight to her dad for a nice rub before coming to me.

"Good morning, Princess. How have you been since the last time I saw you?" I cooed, and she gave me a good sniff before deciding I was worthy enough to rub her white belly. "Good girl."

While I petted her, I felt for her organs in order to assess whether they appeared to be normal and for evidence of discomfort. I also checked the general condition of her hair-coat, which was as I expected, and the same for her skin.

"No signs of excessive oiliness or dryness, no dandruff..." I muttered to myself aloud, more for Tom's benefit than my own.

I grabbed a wriggly toy to play with to check her general

level of alertness and interest in her surroundings and her muscle condition. Everything seemed to be good.

"Look, Coco, what's that on there?" I said, adding a spoonful of cat food to the base of the weighing scales.

Her healthy sense of smell meant she more or less leaped onto the scales.

"That would be the only way you'd get me on a set of scales too," Tom said, chuckling.

Not that he needed to worry about that, I thought. He looked perfectly proportionate, considering his petite frame.

Now I, on the other hand, definitely needed to lose some weight. Despite my height, I'd never been a slim guy, and the stress of moving back to Chester Falls and setting up my practice had me slacking in my meal planning. And that was when I actually had a proper meal. Apparently, eating ice cream while watching old reruns of *The Golden Girls* does not constitute a balanced diet.

"Her weight is ideal for her age," I said. "She's perfectly healthy, Tom."

He let out a visible sigh of relief.

"See, baby? I told you there was no reason to worry," he cooed at Coco, who was back in his arms, resting her head on his shoulder and purring away happily.

"Let's just give her the annual shots, and you'll be good to go."

Despite using my best tricks, Coco was not best pleased with me after getting her shots. Even another spoonful of food didn't convince her I wasn't the evilest human on the planet.

Fortunately for me, she was an extremely social kitten, and I'd bet my degree that she'd run to me for a belly rub the next time I walked past Tom's store, Fabulize.

"Thank you so much, Micah," Tom said when Coco was settled back in her carrier.

"It's my pleasure. See you around."

My schedule looked clear for at least thirty minutes, so I walked to the reception area to see if April wanted me to fix her a coffee while I grabbed a quick lunch upstairs.

I nearly bumped into Tom, who was staring at the walls with a curious look.

"Tom, is everything okay? Did you forget something?"

"Oh, no, I was just memorizing your layout so I can draw you a nice plan."

I smiled. "I don't think I can afford to have any work done out here, Tom. As much as I appreciate—"

A gasp from April made us both turn. She had a paper in her hand and had gone as white as a ghost.

"April, are you okay?"

She looked at me slowly and handed me the paper.

"I was opening today's mail..."

My eyes landed on the words *bankruptcy matter,* and my stomach dropped, making me feel sick. I tried to calm down and read the rest of the letter to make sure I didn't misunderstand the situation.

Please be advised that this firm has been retained to represent the above-referenced debtors for the purposes of bankruptcy filing under Chapter 7 of the United States Bankruptcy Code.

It was all gone. The money my grandad had left me. It was all gone. The contracting company had filed for bankruptcy, and it was unlikely I'd ever see any of that money again.

"Micah, what's going on?" Tom asked, his voice laced with worry.

"I feel so stupid," I said, holding on to the letter as if I could will the words to disappear.

"What do you mean?"

"The contractors said I had to pay for the work up front because they're a small company and couldn't afford to buy the materials before getting paid. I should have known better."

The door to the practice opened, so I turned to go back into the consultation room. I couldn't have my patients see me like this. I needed to pull myself together and think about this later.

A hand on my arm stopped me.

"Hey, it's only Wren. You're among friends," Tom said gently.

I nodded and went over to the chairs in the waiting area and sat down.

"April, can you call up the nearest animal sanctuaries and check what their situation is? We may need to call on them for help. And we'll need to find forever homes for the ones we have in the backyard because we don't have anywhere suitable enough to keep them over the winter months."

"Of course, doctor. I'll get right on it."

Tom sat next to me. "Is there anything we can do to help?"

"No, unless you know of people looking to offer a bunch of perfectly imperfect pets a forever home."

He gave me a wide smile. "Leave it with Uncle Tom."

"Oh, boy," Wren said. "Here we go again."

Tom gave Wren a murderous look, and I managed a laugh when Wren looked terrified, but soon enough, Tom was walking into his arms and asking for lunch.

"Honestly," Wren said to me, "we'll speak to everyone

we can. I see the parents after football practice most days, so I can mention you have some pets up for adoption."

"It's not that easy, Wren. Some of the animals have special needs. That's why they're here and not in someone's home. They were either found abandoned on the side of the road or left here because they have complex medical needs."

"Like I said. We'll do what we can."

I nodded and smiled.

Chester Falls was one of those rare places where people knew and helped each other. Or at least that's how it had been when I was growing up.

I could only hope the same community spirit still prevailed in Chester Falls, because now I had no idea how I could build a weatherproof shelter to keep the animals through winter.

SANTI

"*Look straight ahead. I'm just going to look at the back of your eye,*" *the doctor said.*

The lights were out, so all I could see was the bright light I was meant to be staring at. I was pretty sure last year's exam hadn't taken this long.

"Lieutenant, have you had any issues with night blindness?" he asked.

Well, I'm not a fucking cat, am I? Of course I can't see in the dark.

That's what I wanted to say because the exam was making me antsy, and I had shit to do. But as a lieutenant in the US Army, one that was about to become a captain, I knew better than to be a smartass to the person who was currently standing between me and my promotion.

"Not any more than usual, doctor. We have night-vision equipment, and I can move around camp at night easily enough."

That was if I forgot the time I tripped on a box that was right in front of me. But in my defense, the fucker hadn't been there before, and I'd been drinking with the guys. I hadn't been drunk, by any stretch of the imagination, but I bet someone moved the box to mess with my head.

"Hmm...any blinking or swirling lights?"

I swallowed, feeling suddenly hot under the collar of my uniform.

"Doctor, if you're looking for my soul, you won't find it there." Damn it, Santi. If your mouth fucks this up...

The doctor sat back on this chair and rolled away from the equipment he was using for the eye examination. "I just need to carry out a further test."

He turned the lights back on, and my eyes struggled to adjust. The doctor picked up a handheld device, holding it to my left eye just as everything suddenly went dark.

I woke up with a jolt.

My phone showed five missed calls from my brother, Luca, and five from his boyfriend and my best friend, Ryan.

The phone started ringing again, but I ignored it.

Considering I'd spent the last twelve years in and out of war zones, making split-second decisions, and basically acting like I was a fucking superhero, I'd suddenly become a master of avoidance.

Well, having your career stolen from under your feet for something you can't control does take you down a notch... or five hundred.

The door to my bedroom opened with a jolt, and suddenly I was attacked by one-hundred-and-fifty pounds of wet, slobbery dog tongue.

"Jesus, Duchess. Where the hell have you been? You stink, and now I need to change my sheets...again."

I got up and dragged her to the bathroom. Just what I needed before I'd even had my morning coffee.

The dark-gray Great Dane had been an unrequested gift

from my parents before they decided to move to New Haven.

They'd always loved going to the city to see plays and concerts, so it didn't surprise me when they announced they'd found the perfect apartment within walking distance of the waterfront as well as New Haven's music and arts hub. Just what they wanted in their retirement.

Sometimes I wondered if they'd moved out shortly after I came back home to Chester Falls because of my near-constant moodiness and then decided to give me the three-year-old rescue as revenge.

"Get in the bathtub," I asked.

She howled at me as if saying *no way*. I sighed, struggling to find the energy to handle her.

"Fine. You smell all you like, but you're sleeping outside until you have a bath."

She howled again.

"No arguments. I'm grabbing a coffee, and then we're going for a run so I can feel more human."

If the guys in my unit saw me talking to a dog, they'd find me certifiable. But Duchess was so vocal, it was easy to forget she was a dog.

She sat in front of me as I relieved myself and then brushed my teeth.

"This is not normal, Duchess. A guy needs his privacy."

She replied by resting her head on her front legs.

When I was done in the bathroom, I grabbed my running shorts and a T-shirt, all under the watchful eye of Duchess Olive McPickles, the nosiest dog in the world.

I probably needed to get a book about Great Danes, or large breed dogs, or something. Maybe I should drop by Bookmarked later and check out their books because I was pretty sure Duchess' behavior wasn't normal.

A loud noise came from downstairs, making me groan. "Duchess, why does it sound like there's a duck in my kitchen?"

I stared at her and could swear she shrugged. Fuck, I was going insane.

She followed me downstairs, but as soon as I reached the bottom step, she ran around me, hitting me on the leg with her tail.

"Fuck, that hurts."

I took a deep breath before going into the kitchen, hoping that the sound I heard wasn't a real duck. Not that I could think of any alternatives to what it could be.

As it turned out, the noise did come from a real duck, who was drinking water from Duchess's water bowl after leaving me a nice present right in the middle of the floor.

Yup, this was definitely not normal.

Duchess went around the duck, who seemed unperturbed by the large dog.

"Seriously, Duchess? You're afraid of peeing in the dark, but you're not afraid of a duck? And where the fuck did you find a duck?"

Okay, one thing at a time.

I got the coffee machine going then scooped up the poop before leading the duck to the backyard. He or she would be safe there until I figured out what to do.

Duchess stared at me and then her water bowl.

"What? You want more water? The bowl is half-full."

I filled up her food bowl, but she refused to eat anything until I added more water to the bowl.

Talk about a bowl-half-empty kind of dog.

"Here we go again," I muttered to myself as I left the house to knock on the neighbors' doors.

It only took me three attempts to realize that asking if

someone lost a pet duck was only going to be met with strange looks.

Fortunately, the third person I spoke to gave me the phone number for the local vet clinic.

I'd already written off my run and definitely needed some food to go with the coffee that I hadn't drunk yet.

Duchess was a very social dog, so normally I took her out with me every time I left the house, and when I didn't, I could count on her standing by the door waiting for me with the sole purpose of giving me the stink eye.

This time, however, there was no greeting, which could only mean one thing.

There was trouble in the kitchen.

I steeled myself to find a cat, a chicken, or, god forbid, a goat in my kitchen as I followed the corridor.

Okay, so there were no other strange animals. Just Duchess sleeping on her bed with the duck cuddled up to her, also sleeping.

On my to-do list, closing the dog flap to the backyard was now a priority. Duchess could learn to call me if she wanted to go out. The thing was getting too small for her anyway.

I popped a piece of bread in the toaster and filled a cup with coffee.

With my now-late breakfast on the kitchen table, I took out the number for the vet and called them up.

"Chester Falls Vets, this is April. How can I help?"

"Hi...um, I have a situation here, and I need some advice."

"Is the animal in distress?" she asked.

I looked at the dog and duck in front of me.

"Definitely not," I chuckled.

"Excellent, what is the situation?"

"My dog brought home a duck."

There was a moment of silence. I looked at the phone and saw the call was still connected.

"Excuse me?" she asked.

"I came downstairs this morning, and my dog had brought a duck in. I don't know what to do."

"What is the duck doing now?"

"Um..." I closed my eyes and scrunched up my face, ready for the call to get disconnected. "The duck is asleep with my dog on her bed."

"Oh, well, this is good news," she said.

"It is?"

"Yes, ducks protect you from negative emotions and help you get ready to accept and experience human relationships. Ducks will help you become a healthy and loving human."

Did she just...huh?

"I'm sorry, is there a veterinarian I can speak to?"

"Oh, of course. I'll call Doctor Sawyer for you."

I remembered the old town vet. My brother and I'd had a gerbil when we were kids, but it died prematurely. Doctor Sawyer had been great with us, but we'd been too upset to ever consider having another pet.

She put me on hold, and a moment later, I was greeted by a soft, smooth voice that didn't sound at all like Doctor Sawyer, who must have been, what, eighty?

"Hello, this is Doctor Sawyer. My assistant tells me you have a ducking situation?"

I snorted and looked at my phone, sad that I couldn't see the old doctor because I wanted to hear him say those words with a straight face.

"Yes, I guess I do have a ducking situation."

"So, about your duck...are you keeping it?"

"What? I can't keep a duck," I said. My voice going up a few decibels.

"Where's the duck again?" he asked.

"Sleeping with my dog in the..." Fuck. "Yeah, I guess I'm keeping the ducking duck."

He laughed, and for some reason, that sound made me feel happy.

"Do you have an email address?" he asked.

"Yes?" Why did he want my email?

"You do? Or you're not sure you do?"

"I do."

He laughed again as I spelled out my email.

"I will send you a document with some information about keeping ducks as pets. If you have any questions, you can always call me...I mean, the clinic. You can always call this number...for the clinic."

I couldn't erase the smile off my face after the call was finished, even when I realized my coffee was now cold and the toast untouched.

MICAH

"Hi, Micah, what can I get you?" Indy, the owner of Spilled Beans, asked from behind the counter filled with delicious pastries.

I smiled as I scanned through to find the exact pastry that would magically lift my spirits through its sugary and flavorful goodness.

"A cinnamon roll to go, please."

It was a beautiful day. Not a cloud in the sky, not even a small breeze.

I'd spent the morning in the backyard, cleaning the mess from the rescue animals and feeding them. After a cool shower, I'd decided to get out for a walk.

Losing my money to the contractors had been on my mind, so I'd hoped a walk and some fresh air would do me good, not to mention I desperately needed some form of exercise.

I knew I shouldn't spend money on a pastry, but hell, it's not like I could even buy a single brick for the price of the treat. And damn, Indy's cinnamon rolls were to die for.

So no, I couldn't regret giving myself the small reward for a week of hard work, especially after the news I'd had.

I crossed the bridge over the river to get onto the path leading back to my car, eating bites of the cinnamon roll as I admired the ducks sitting on the bank.

I thought of the guy who had called the clinic a few days ago.

The whole conversation was so bizarre that I'd put the phone down, certain it had been a joke.

On the off chance that it wasn't, I had still sent him some information about ducks and a couple of useful links. He'd replied, thanking me for the help. He'd even included a photo of his dog cuddling up to the duck.

To say the two animals were adorable together was an understatement. It was a shame their owner hadn't included himself in the photo.

He had a deep voice that had the potential to reach all the hidden corners of someone's soul. Assertive but gentle.

I had such a weak spot for guys who liked animals, and even if he was reluctantly adopting the duck, in my mind, he was already one hundred percent hotter by default.

From the sound of his voice, I thought he was either around my age or maybe a little older, but no more than his mid-thirties. I imagined he was tall with dark hair that was maybe overdue for a cut and perfect to hold on to when being kissed.

I finished my cinnamon bun, feeling happier from the sugar high and a little hornier from thinking about the duck man.

God, I needed to do something about my lack of sex life, or love life, or a life in general.

Coming back to Chester Falls had been a fresh start for

me, so I was going to put on my big-boy pants and find someone to date or even just a hookup.

I needed to end this dry spell for good.

Was it even a dry spell if you'd never been with anyone? It wasn't as if I'd ever had a wet spell.

Maybe it was just a spell? Whatever it was, it needed to end before I went into my thirties a pathetic virgin.

My parents had already given me plenty of hints that they were ready to be grandparents or see me in a settled relationship. As if I didn't want that too. Getting it was the hard part.

Being away from home for the duration of my studies, plus an extra two years, meant they'd never questioned my lack of mentioning any boyfriends. They probably thought I'd dated throughout college and vet school and needed to settle down now.

If only they knew.

If only it was as easy to talk to real-life men as it was to communicate with the animals I worked with. Animals, I understood. People, and in particular, men, not so much.

Lost in my thoughts, I didn't notice I was veering toward the middle of the path. One moment I was upright, inside my own head and throwing myself an awesome pity party, and the next, I was no longer upright but on my hands and knees, precariously close to falling into the river.

What the fuck?

The guy that bumped into me only spared a quick look as if to check I wasn't face-down on the path or in the river. Since I was neither, he carried on.

Well, thank you for stopping, asshole.

With my heart very close to my throat, I sat on the grassy edge of the path to get my wits back.

Deep breaths. At least you've already had the pastry, or

you would have lost it alongside your pride, and that would have been a real shame.

I wrapped my arms around my legs and rested my head on my knees, closing my eyes for a moment. The adrenaline of being pushed over was wearing off, and my throat was starting to close up.

The last thing I needed was for all the stress of the last few days to come out via an ugly cry on a public path.

Something wet nudged against my neck, and I looked up to find myself staring at a Great Dane.

She licked my face and then plopped herself onto my lap, forcing me to stretch my legs so she could lay across them before raising her head for a scratch.

As the trained human I was, I couldn't help myself and did as she asked. I was even rewarded with more licks.

My mood instantly lifted. Evidence, if I'd ever needed any, that I was so much better with animals than people.

"Pickles, no!"

My eyes followed the voice, who was clearly calling out to the dog that had claimed me as a couch.

As soon as I laid eyes on the tower of man approaching, I knew this was going to be awkward.

Because A: he was tall, B: he was hot, and C: he was totally my type, which meant I was about to embarrass myself. As if I hadn't done enough of that by getting myself nearly pushed into the river.

"Pickles, what are you rescuing now? We're not taking it home," the guy said. His voice sounded familiar, but he was wearing sunglasses while in front of the sun, which made it harder to see.

I tried to stand up, but the heavy dog made it impossible.

"What have you got—oh." The guy crouched near me, looking as surprised to see me under his dog as I was.

"Hi, I'm sorry. Did she knock you over?" he asked.

His voice was laced with worry as if he were already trying to make up for whatever misdemeanor his dog had caused.

"No, I...um, I was already down here."

"Phew, that's good. I'm not sure I have space at home for a full-size rescue human, and you wouldn't fit through the dog flap." He smiled a perfect white smile that made my stomach tighten.

I opened my mouth, hoping to say something smart or witty but was cut off by a duck coming around the guy and settling next to the dog's head.

"If a bird lands on me now, I'll seriously consider the option that when I was knocked over, I knocked myself out, and now I'm having Snow White dreams. Although, knowing my luck, I'd get bird poop on my head rather than an actual bird," I muttered to myself, wondering what the hell was happening.

The guy laughed aloud and pushed his glasses up on his head. His eyes were dark and deep. The kind of eyes that could suck you right in and have you lost to the world for hours.

I had to look away before I said something stupid, so I looked down at my new friend.

"You called her Pickles. Is that her name?" I asked, running my hand over the dog's shiny coat.

"Her full name is Duchess Olive McPickles. She answers to whatever the hell she likes, so I call her by the first thing that comes out."

"And how about this guy here?" I asked, pointing to the duck.

"That one is a recent addition to the family and doesn't have a name because I don't know what it is."

"He's a duck," I said before I bit my lip to stop myself.

The guy laughed. "I gathered as much." And then he leaned closer and whispered, "I don't know if it's a boy or a girl."

It was my turn to laugh. "He's a male duck, also known as a drake...wait...you're...she's...he's..." I pointed to each in turn. "You're the duck guy?"

He stared at me, confused.

"I'm the vet. Are you the guy who called about the duck?" I asked.

"Yes. You're...Doctor Sawyer? But you're not old."

I did a doubletake. What did he...oh...

"I'm the other Doctor Sawyer, but please, call me Micah. My grandad passed away a few years ago. I reopened his practice last year."

He nodded.

"So what are you going to call him?" I asked.

He shrugged. "No clue. I was hoping by bringing him out on a walk, we'd find his natural family, but he seems totally enamored with Olive and has ignored every single duck that we've walked past."

"I think he looks like a Gus," I said without thinking. "Oh, sorry, I didn't mean to..."

"No, I like it. Gus it is. And I'm Santi, by the way."

Santi?

If I was already feeling hot all over from the presence of the super-hot, super-tall, totally-my-type guy, now I was definitely going to evaporate.

"Santi as in...Santiago Torres?"

"Yes, have we met?" His eyes narrowed as if he was trying to remember.

"No...we went to the same school, but we were in different grades. You were a few years ahead of me."

Not to mention the object of my total infatuation.

He cocked his head. "Actually, I think I remember you."

"You do?"

I'd been one of the invisible kids throughout school. Not cool or good-looking enough to be with the cool kids, not smart enough to be with the geeks, or creative enough to be with the music and art kids. I'd mostly gone through school dreaming of finishing it so I could become a vet. It was all I'd ever wanted to do.

How did Santi Torres notice me?

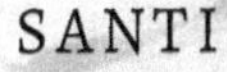

"I do. You were in my brother's class, right?"

How could I have not remembered him? Even back in high school, he was adorable. With his blond hair, bright green eyes, and full lips, I'd always thought he was beautiful. There was something about him that drew my attention whenever I saw him walk past, holding his backpack on one shoulder and seemingly lost in his own world.

"Luca. Yeah, I was in his class. How is he? I haven't seen him around," he said.

"He's in Lydovia. He does security work with his boyfriend out there. Remember Ryan?"

Micah nodded. "Yeah, I do. You mean they're together? But I thought..." He didn't finish his sentence, so I finished it for him.

"That Ryan and I were together?" I laughed at the ridiculous thought. There had never been a moment in our lives when Ryan and I felt more than friendship for each other. He was my wingman, my brother-in-arms, and hopefully soon, he'd be my brother-in-law.

Another nod. Micah kept his attention on Olive as we spoke and only rarely met my gaze. Was he shy? I knew I could look intimidating because of my height and size, which was the reason I'd crouched beside him.

Micah had always been a mystery to me, and now, looking at the adult version, part of me regretted not approaching him years ago. I'd always been too focused on playing sports and being fit enough to follow my dream of serving in the military.

"Ryan's my best friend, but he was always meant to be with Luca. I'm just happy they finally found each other," I said.

"How about you?" he asked, raising his head a little as if he wanted to look at me but didn't dare.

Good question, Micah.

"Me? I'm a free agent."

"Of course, I didn't mean to pry...I shouldn't have...." Micah met my gaze. His green eyes were intense but warm. "I should probably go."

Already?

"Yeah, us too. These guys will want food soon." I patted Olive. "Come on, Duchess. You too, Gus."

Gus raised his head from where it was resting against Olive, and she also seemed reluctant to let go of Micah, and I wasn't sure if I could blame them at all.

Micah was round, soft, and gentle. His full beard looked silky, and I could only imagine what it would be like to feel it and his body against mine.

Stop it, Santi.

I stood and held my hand out to help him up.

He moved to take my hand, but at the last minute, withdrew it. "It's okay. I can do it."

We stood there staring at each other awkwardly until I broke the silence.

"Nice to finally meet you, Micah."

"Same here... If you ever have any questions, give me a shout," he said.

"That's a generous offer. I always have many questions... about lots of things..." I smiled, unable to resist teasing the cute vet.

"Um...of course...about the pets, I mean...um...see ya..."

And with that, Micah Sawyer left me standing by the river with my two weird as fuck pets while staring at his round ass, soft waist, and broad back. The man was everything I shouldn't want, but fuck me, I wouldn't say no if he ever wanted to have some fun.

Even though it took me a long time to figure out why I wanted to kiss boys as much as I wanted to kiss girls, I'd gotten the distinct impression, even in high school, that Micah was gay. The fact that he'd assumed I'd be with Ryan and that he remembered me were positive signs that I'd been right.

Or maybe it was wishful thinking.

As soon as we got home, I was summoned by Mr. and Mrs. Bossy to fill up the water bowl because, apparently, a gallon isn't enough for Pickles. The bowl *must* be full at all times.

I put some food in their bowls too, which, fortunately, they didn't share, and then made myself a sandwich. It was time to tackle the mail I'd been dreading for the best part of a week.

The various tests I'd done over the last few months had all confirmed what the VA ophthalmologist had diagnosed.

Retinitis pigmentosa. Two words I'd never heard before but had the power to change my life.

None of the doctors I'd seen outside of the VA could give me any more information than I'd gotten in the diagnosis.

I put the letters down, noticing one that didn't have a stamp. I ignored that one since it was probably some kind of local stuff I wouldn't be interested in anyway.

Olive nudged my arm.

"What's up, girl?"

She made a bunch of sounds as if she was talking to me, and then she licked my hand.

Gus went out to the backyard through the dog flap. I shook my head, wondering if this was really my life.

"I don't speak your language, Pickles," I said, turning back to her.

Her bowl of water was full, and I knew she wasn't hungry. She did a few jumps to the couch and then back to me.

"Oh, I gotcha. Why didn't you say so?" I went over to the couch and sat at one end. She jumped up and lay down, taking over the rest of the space with her head and front paws on my lap.

"Didn't you get enough petting from the hot vet earlier?" I asked, rubbing her coat. "I wouldn't have minded the same treatment, you lucky girl."

Her reply was another growl type of communication. Since my parents adopted her for me, I'd been reading up on the breed to make sure I didn't do something that was unintentionally harmful to her.

Apparently, Great Danes loved talking. Well, their own version of talking. Which also came hand-in-hand with a ridiculous amount of slobber. I now kept small towels everywhere in the house, especially in the kitchen, where she drank her water.

At some point, I must have fallen asleep because I woke up to the sound of my phone ringing. And I must have been really out of it because my thumb slid across the screen before I could even think about what I was doing.

"Santi, what the fuck are you playing at?" my brother's angry voice shouted in my ear.

I groaned.

"What do you mean?"

There were some muffled noises before Ryan came on the phone.

"Dude, your brother has been worried sick, and so have I. Why aren't you answering your phone?"

"I've been busy."

"And you couldn't find five minutes in your busy schedule to call us back? What gives?"

I knew I couldn't bullshit him. I loved him and my brother too much. But I was still trying to accept my condition, which meant it felt too soon to tell them about it. There would be questions I couldn't answer, the same ones I was still trying to find answers for.

I also knew they wouldn't stop hounding until I gave them something.

"Can you put me on loudspeaker?" I asked.

"Okay, you're on," he said.

"I've left the military."

"You think we haven't gathered as much? You haven't been home this long in years," Luca said, his voice still carrying an edge. "The question is, what the hell happened? You've worked your whole life for this, and you were on the verge of a promotion."

Thanks for the reminder, bro.

I closed my eyes and rubbed the lids with the heels of

my hands. When I opened them, all I could see were floating spots until my vision was restored.

"Things change. I changed. Maybe I want to fuck someone more than once before I leave them behind. Maybe I want to enjoy my fucking life without fearing it'll be cut short by some extremist," I said, failing to take the edge off my voice.

There were two sighs on the other side of the phone. I knew they didn't believe my bullshit. Santi Torres was a *fuck 'em and leave 'em* kind of guy. Santi Torres thrived in a war zone.

But the war I was fighting now was one I'd never expected, and it was one I'd eventually lose.

Fuck this depressing shit.

"Hey, did you know The Falls has a new owner, and it's been redecorated with darker woods, leather seats, hot bartenders, and plenty of hidden corners?" I said, changing the subject. "Ryan, man, it's the perfect place to find a willing body for some stress relief."

"Ryan does not need anyone to help him relieve stress," my brother bit back, and I laughed.

"How's Zeke? Does he miss me much?" I said in a teasing voice.

Zeke was one of Lydovia's royal family guards, just like Ryan and Luca. When I'd visited them at Christmas, just as they were on the verge of getting together, Zeke had volunteered to show me around.

He'd been a fun guy to hang out with, and he'd made it clear on more than one occasion that he'd happily help me out with my own stress relief. As much as that had been tempting, I hadn't wanted to make things awkward for my brother and Ryan.

There was no chance Zeke would be more than a

hookup for me, and I actually liked the guy enough to keep him as a friend.

"I'm not talking to him," Luca said.

"Why not?"

Ryan chuckled. "Because every time Luca walks past, Zeke looks at his crotch, says your name, and then lets out a sigh." He choked, no doubt after getting punched in the stomach by my brother, and I laughed.

"Zeke's a weird dude, but he's good people. You know I didn't actually hook up with him, right?" I asked.

"Yeah, we know. I'm his boss. I've seen his medical files, and he's STD-free," Ryan said.

"Fuck you, Ry Ry."

"No thanks. I'd rather fuck your brother."

"And on that note," Luca said.

"Ew, gross. I don't ever want that image in my head. I'm going now."

There was a moment of silence, so I assumed they'd started eating each other's faces before disconnecting the call. Rude.

But then my brother spoke. "You know we're here for you, right, Santi? We can come home any time."

"I know, Luc." I took a deep breath. "I'm still adjusting to civilian life, but this is what I need. And if you ever have a moment where you're not jumping each other's bones, I'll visit you."

"Unlikely," Ryan said, and I heard shuffling on the other side.

I ended the call before I had to cut off my own ears.

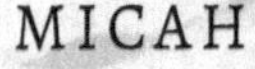

MICAH

$\mathcal{M}$y back ached, and I'd found muscles I didn't know I had, but it was the kind of pleasant soreness you normally get from a workout.

If I worked out, that is. The last time I remembered being inside a gym was in high school.

Not that I was a stranger to back-breaking work. During vet school, I worked on many farms with larger animals. There was nothing quite like helping a cow birth a calf or chasing a sheep in an enclosed compound.

This time, however, my work hadn't involved any animals.

Since I'd lost the money for the sanctuary, I'd decided to take matters into my own hands. There was no other option. Even if it meant a few more hours of work every day.

My grandad had built the enormous barn behind the house with the hope of building his own animal shelter one day. Unfortunately, between the work at his practice and my grandmother's illness, he'd never had a chance to make it happen.

I guess at some point, he figured it was too late, so he'd used the barn for storage.

After spending my last day off going through a lot of the stuff inside the barn, I'd uncovered some useful things. Alongside other very useless things, but that was Grandad for you. Everything could come in handy, so he never threw anything out.

I was hopeful that if I could clear it all out over the summer that I'd be able to use it for the animals. It wasn't ideal, but it was better than having them outdoors during the cold winter months.

After checking my schedule, I locked my computer and grabbed my wallet and car keys.

"April, I don't have any appointments for the rest of the day, so I'm going to the general store to buy some supplies."

"No problem, Doctor Sawyer. I'll call if anything happens."

Masons, the Chester Falls general store, had a little bit of everything. From feed for animals to household essentials, they seemed to cover what the grocery store didn't have. And since New Haven was at least a thirty-minute drive, having a good supply store in town was perfect.

Troy, the Mason's youngest son, was behind the checkout desk when I walked in.

"Hey, Troy. How's it going?"

Troy had only been a little kid when I left for college, so when I moved back, I almost didn't recognize him.

"Great, thanks. Hey, Micah, can I come to your place again next week?"

"Sure, your help is always appreciated, and I think the animals love you," I said. Troy had found a stray dog on the side of the road a couple of months ago and brought it to the clinic to get checked.

He couldn't keep it because his mom was allergic, but since then, he liked to come by to see the animals and volunteer with anything that needed doing.

"I'd like to go there more often, but I'm helping out my parents here during summer break. Anyway, is there anything I can get you?"

"Yes, please. If you can get me a bag of pellets, two boxes of dog food, one of cat food, and a bag of corn, that would be great. I'll go browse while you get them. I also need a few of those cheap blankets you have. Mindy could give birth any day now, and I haven't got any nice blankets for her and the kittens."

Troy's eyes opened wide. "Oh man, I'd love to have a kitten. It sucks that Mom is allergic."

"You can come visit her as often as you like. I'll even give you naming rights."

He gave me a bright, blue-eyed smile and went to the back to get my stuff.

I walked over to the aisle where they kept pet supplies but stopped in my tracks when I saw none other than Santi Torres standing there, looking all tall and gorgeous.

It had been a few days since we'd met on the river path after I was knocked over by that jackass.

Santi had been kind and gentle, checking if I was okay. His pets were ridiculously adorable, which, of course, increased his sexiness rate by a million. About the same rate my awkwardness increased by too.

"Micah," he said, a wide smile spreading over his face, reaching his eyes, and making my stomach tighten a little.

"Santi." My words were stuck in my throat, and my palms felt sweaty.

Why couldn't I be normal around a guy I found attractive? It's not like the feeling was mutual. He probably thought I was weird and awkward as fuck. Which was sadly very accurate.

"Are you buying supplies?" he asked.

"Um, yeah...I have a few rescue dogs, cats, chickens, and a goat at the clinic. Mindy's about to have her kittens, and Poppy escaped out of her enclosure and decided to eat the blankets, so now I need some blankets and extra feeding bowls because—" I stopped myself there for two reasons.

One, I was very aware that I was rambling and needed to shut up, and two, there was a strange sound coming from Santi.

I didn't think Santi was the kind of guy that blushed or looked unsure of himself, but as the sound came out of him again, I could swear there was a little bit of pink trying to peak out from the collar of his shirt.

"What's that?" I asked.

"What's what?"

"That noise."

"What noise?" he asked, just in time for it to happen again, and this time, because I wasn't rambling, I heard it properly.

"Do you have a kitten with you?"

"No," he said all too quickly.

"So...that sound coming from your clothes is...?"

"I'm hungry. It's my belly. I didn't have breakfast this morning because Pickles stole it."

I actually laughed aloud. "You do realize you're talking to a vet, right?"

His shoulders sagged, and he looked around before pulling down the zipper on his sweater to show a kitten that couldn't be more than four weeks old.

I instinctively went to grab it, but the kitten was literally attached to Santi, and it was almost impossible to get the claws out of his shirt. Since Troy's mom was allergic, and there were other customers around the store, I didn't want to draw attention to Santi and his precious cargo, so I let go.

"Olive brought it in the other day and put it on her bed," Santi said, sounding exasperated. "I don't know how to stop that dog from bringing things home. She's a fucking kleptomaniac."

"Great Danes are very social creatures, so it's not unusual to see them bond with other animals."

"Yeah, but she's afraid to pee outside when it's raining. How is she not afraid of this razor-sharp weapon that you're calling a kitten?"

I laughed and reached out again to the kitten to check the sex. "You've got another boy on your hands. Olive clearly has a preference. Where's the mom? Are there any siblings?"

Santi's face dropped. "She's dead. Same with the three siblings. After Olive brought him in, she kept whining and asking me to follow her. She took me to the back of this abandoned building, where the mom looked like she'd been attacked by something. The kittens were next to her."

I ran my fingers over the white-and-gray stripes on the kitten's fur. "They may have died of dehydration. Has this little one drank anything?"

"Yeah, I put a plate with water in front of him, and he drank, but I have no idea what to feed him."

"He looks around four weeks old, so he'll need formula mixed with cat food. If you bring him to the clinic, I can check his health."

I took out my wallet and gave him a card with the contact and address details for the clinic.

"Can you tell me where you found the mom? I can

check if she's microchipped. The kitten may belong to someone who's looking for the mom."

Santi nodded. "She's near my place. I can bring her over to you if that's easier."

"Sure."

He still looked a little lost, so I grabbed a basket and put some essentials in it before handing it to him.

"Here. This should do until you know if you can keep him."

"Thanks."

There were many things in life I was unsure about or did wrong. Case in point, the money I lost to the contractors, which I now knew should never have been paid upfront. But there was one area I excelled: my job as a veterinarian.

I left Santi to finish his shopping and grabbed a basket for myself before looking for the blankets. If I could keep talking to Santi about his pets, I might stop sounding like a total loser.

He thanked me before leaving the store, promising to drop by the clinic later.

There was no way I'd shut the clinic until Santi came over, so I sent April home and sat at the reception desk doing some admin while I waited.

It was close to seven when Santi arrived. He had a box in his hand and a satchel across his body, where the kitten's head peeked out with curiosity.

I went around the desk to open the door, making sure to lock it after him.

"Did you walk here? I don't see a car outside."

"Yeah, I don't drive," he said, following me to the exam room.

He walked around the room holding the kitten and

reading the various information posters I had on the walls. I didn't blame him for not wanting to watch me check the mom for the microchip.

"She's not tagged, so it's up to you if you want to keep him. I have a new mom about to give birth, so she'd probably take him in."

I closed the box with the cat and her deceased kittens and took it to the freezer to wait for the next crematorium collection.

When I turned back to Santi, he was holding the invite I'd had on my desk.

"You got this too?" he asked.

"The invite to Mr. Baxter's memorial dedication?"

"Yeah."

Mr. Baxter had been the high school principal when I went to school in Chester Falls. He'd retired early because he had cancer. It seemed he'd still had a few good years before he passed away last year.

"Are you going?" Santi asked.

"I don't know. I want to go but...I probably won't know anyone there, and I'm not too good with people, but Mr. Baxter was really nice, so I should go. After all, it's not every day you get to witness part of your old school being named after someone you actually knew."

"I doubt that," he said, cocking his head.

"Doubt what?"

"That you're not good with people."

I laughed. "You met me after I'd been pushed onto the river bank by a runner. If that isn't *not* being a people person, I don't know what is."

"I'm glad Olive found you," he said, his dark eyes boring into me.

I wanted to tell him I was also glad Olive found me, but

I was too afraid that my mouth would say something stupid like he could keep me too.

He lifted the kitten to meet his face and got a lick as a reward.

"You're the last one. No more," he said to the kitten.

Somehow, I doubted that would remain true.

SANTI

There wasn't a single empty space in the high-school parking lot, and that was in addition to the number of people I'd seen walk from town on my way here.

Crowds never used to scare me, but now I was more than a little apprehensive at being around so many people. My peripheral vision was starting to fail sometimes, especially when I was tired, and I found it difficult to go from well-lit to darker places and vice versa.

I kept reaching out to my side, only to remember I'd left Olive at home, babysitting Gus and the kitten I'd named Alfie.

I wondered if Micah was already inside the large school gym.

His words at the clinic about not being good with people had stayed with me well after I'd left him. So Micah really was shy.

There was something about him that fiercely drew me in, and from the conversations I'd overheard the few times

I'd gone to Spilled Beans for one of Indy's amazing cakes, I was certain other people liked him too.

Maybe he just couldn't see it.

He was warm, kind, and helpful.

The day I'd found Alfie, it had taken me a while to figure out how to carry both him and the box. I'd underestimated how long it would take me to walk the distance from my place, so I'd arrived later than I'd wanted.

I knew he didn't have to keep the clinic open to examine Alfie and check out his mom, but he'd done it anyway.

Micah's advice on how to feed Alfie had been a lifesaver, and I swear the kitten had grown in the two weeks I'd had him.

Olive treated Alfie as if he was her kid, and Alfie treated Olive and Gus as if they were both his own personal sleeping pillow. As for Gus, I had my doubts as to what kind of animal he thought he was because he followed both Olive and Alfie around, liked to sleep wherever it was sunny, and quacked to ask for food.

If my brother and Ryan saw me now, they'd think I've gone mad.

Some days I wasn't sure there was anything of the old Santi left. The old Santi would never have pets, let alone a combination of dog, cat, and duck. I mean, what the actual fuck?

I walked inside the school gym where we used to gather for assemblies. This was the building they were renaming, which was quite apt since Mr. Baxter had spent so much time here giving speeches about the value of education, not giving up on our dreams, and telling us it was okay to fail because we could always learn something from it.

It was dark inside, or at least that's how it looked to me.

I took a deep breath and went in, hoping my memory served me well and I could walk in unnoticed and stand against the wall by the door.

Everyone went silent when the current principal started her speech.

As the ceremony went on, my eyes adjusted to the dimmer light and my vision returned to normal.

I looked around to see if I recognized anyone, but apart from a handful of people I'd seen around at school, there were no old friends. At least that I'd remembered.

I'd enlisted as soon as I could and hadn't been back to Chester Falls except for the few times my breaks between deployments coincided with the holidays.

That was a relief because even though I hadn't really kept in touch with my friends from school, they knew I'd gone into the military. Answering questions about my presence in Chester Falls was not something I wanted to do today.

In fact, I was a lot more interested in seeing the only person that made me feel like I could still be the old Santi.

Micah sat on the bleachers near the podium, wearing a pair of jeans and a dark shirt. His light hair was longer than the first time I'd seen him on the river path. He ran his hands through it as he spoke to the woman sitting next to him.

I instantly regretted not arriving earlier because I could have sat next to him.

The ceremony drew to an end with the plaque unveiling, declaring the gym officially named after Mr. Baxter. The principal informed everyone that there were refreshments available for anyone wanting to stay on to remember Mr. Baxter.

I kept my eyes on Micah, who suddenly seemed to not

know what to do with himself. I thought he might just leave, in which case I'd stay put and wait for him to come to me, but instead, he pulled his phone out and started tapping on the screen.

A few people left the hall, but there was still plenty milling around. I made my way to Micah, following the wall around the gym, which seemed a far more efficient route than crossing the room. And far less dangerous.

I stopped by the refreshments table to grab two drinks, which was when I heard Micah's name.

"I didn't know he was back. Looks like he inherited his pop's place and reopened the vet clinic," a woman said.

"I guess that's one way to start a business. Having it handed down. I'm not sure I'd trust him with my Princess. He wasn't exactly known for being super-smart in high school," another added.

"Smart or good-looking. God, did you see the state of him? Talk about freshman fifteen. More like fifteen per year." The comment came from someone I thought I'd briefly hooked up with at school. The idea that I'd been close to someone who was spouting such hate on Micah made me feel sick.

They all sniggered, and then, not caring if they were within earshot of anyone else, they continued.

"Hey, isn't he gay?"

"Don't know. Never saw him with anyone at school. He's probably still a virgin. I mean, would you want to wake up to that?"

"Hell no."

The more they talked, the more I wanted to punch something and tell them to mind their own business and stop being rude. However, Micah seemed like the kind of person who kept to himself. He wouldn't want a scene when today was about remembering an old teacher.

But I'd be damned if I wasn't itching for a fight.

I walked away to stop myself from doing something I'd regret.

Fortunately, Micah was still looking adorably lost and focusing on his phone as if it were a life raft.

I sat next to him, and when he realized he wasn't on his own, he looked up. His face lit up straight away with a wide smile that made his green eyes look brighter. He also looked relieved.

Had he been waiting for me?

"You came," he said.

"So did you. Juice?" I asked, handing over the plastic cup.

"Thank you. What did you think of the ceremony?"

I hadn't paid much attention because I'd been staring at him, but I couldn't exactly say that.

"I didn't realize Mr. Baxter had a snail collection," I said.

Micah snorted. "*That's* what you took from the whole speech?"

"Hey, when you own a dog who keeps kidnapping random animals, you tell me if you don't suddenly become tuned to anything pet-related."

God, I wanted to tell those women they were so wrong. Just being with Micah made me feel so much better. He had this calmness about him.

I also wanted to rattle him. I wondered what it would take to make the hot doctor even hotter.

"Speaking of your dog, how is everyone? Have you adopted any more pets? It's been two whole weeks since I first saw you, so by all accounts, I'm guessing you now have a pig, two goats, and a pony."

I bumped his shoulder. "I like your sense of humor, Doctor Sawyer, but you're wrong...well, partially wrong, anyway."

He turned in his chair to face me. "I gotta hear this."

"So, last week she brought—"

"Santi? Is that you?"

I looked up to see who'd interrupted us so rudely and found myself staring at two of the women who were talking about Micah earlier. My skin prickled, and I slid a little closer to him on the bench.

"I'm sorry, have we met?" I asked.

Her face dropped a little, but she disguised it well. "We dated senior year."

"Oh, Patty, right?" I asked, getting her name purposefully wrong.

"Jenny," she corrected. "Anyway, are you back in town? I could show you around."

I didn't like the way her eyes roamed my body. It made me want to shower with bleach.

"Actually, Jessie, I already have someone to show me around," I said, getting even closer to Micah.

If she didn't get the message soon, I was going to need a more drastic measure.

"Who? Everyone from high school is already married."

I couldn't even begin to unpack her statement because it was wrong on so many levels, but it also showed how small her world was.

How dare she speak about Micah the way she had earlier?

She stared at me, waiting for an answer, so I put my arm around Micah and pulled him closer, trying to ignore how amazing he felt.

He looked at me with wide eyes but didn't say anything.

At least not with his delectable mouth or expressive eyes. His body, however, had melted into mine as if it knew it was meant to be there.

We'd get to that later. First, I needed to get rid of the high school bully.

I looked back at her with a fake smile, and she finally got it.

Took you long enough.

"Him? You're with him? You're...gay?" She laughed.

I'd seen my fair share of homophobia in the military, but I'd never seen anyone look at another human being the same way she looked at Micah and me.

Micah himself had his eyes fixed on the floor. His body was tense, and the way he had his hands clenched together told me he'd rather be cleaning pig shit than be here.

"Actually, Peggy, I don't owe you my sexual identity or my time. If you could leave us alone, that would be great."

Her face changed completely to show her true colors. "Good luck with that," she said, pointing her chin at Micah. "And that's if he ever puts out. Last I heard, he was still a virgin. Maybe he's saving himself for someone special, or he's in a cult. You should be careful with the likes of him. Never know who he's going to trick next."

I stood, towering her over. "Unless you want to be dragged out of here by your hair extensions, I suggest you and your friend leave now."

She opened her mouth to say something, but her friend seemed to have more sense and took her away by the arm.

I sat again. "Fuck. I've never wanted to hit someone so much, and I've spent twelve years fighting terrorists."

Beside me, I felt Micah let out a long breath before he stood and started walking toward the door.

"Micah, wait."

MICAH

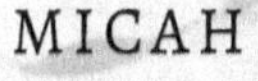

*K*eep *walking, Micah, and don't make eye contact with anyone.*

Never had I been so thankful for getting the time wrong and arriving early at an event because my car wasn't parked far away, and I needed to get out of here.

I'd have jumped into a hole if one had appeared in front of me, but since that didn't happen, the second-best thing was to avoid speaking to anyone before I was able to reach the car and leave.

How fucking embarrassing.

Now Santi knew exactly how much of a loser I'd always been. And the fact he felt he had to pretend to be with me to get rid of the bullies made it even worse.

I was never going to be able to look him in the face again.

"Micah, wait!"

Great, here comes the awkward cherry on top of the fucking embarrassment sundae.

"Sorry, Santi, I remembered I have to go back to the clinic. I'll see you around," I said without turning.

"Micah, please..." His voice sounded off, and like the sucker for punishment I was, I stopped. Santi was looking around, rubbing his eyes and facing the wrong way even though I was only about five yards away from him.

"Santi?" He looked in my direction, but his eyes weren't focused on me, so I broke the distance.

As soon as I was close enough, he pulled me into his arms.

"Fuck, don't do that again," he said gruffly.

His chest was rock hard and his arms tight. I kept mine by my side because I didn't dare trust myself if I touched him.

"Do...what?" I asked, trying not to be too obvious about smelling him because damn...

Stop it, Micah.

"Don't run where I can't see you."

"What do you mean?"

"Can you take me to the bench under the tree? I saw it on the way in," he said.

"Sure."

I knew which bench he meant. It was off to the side of the building, closer to the classrooms. With the school shut for the summer and most people either inside of the gym or leaving to go home, the bench was fairly private.

I held his hand and walked us away from the gym building.

When we sat down, Santi was shaking. His face was unreadable, but his body was as tense as I'd ever seen anyone.

"Are you okay?" I asked.

"Yeah...I just...it takes a moment for my eyes to adjust to the light, and when I couldn't see you..." He let out a breath. "Fuck, I can't do this."

I wasn't sure what to say, so I let him calm down.

After a minute, he turned to me and placed his big, strong hands on either side of my face. His eyes were dead-focused on me now, as if he were trying to memorize every inch of my face.

I smiled, and he smiled back, running his thumb over my bottom lip.

Sirens were going off inside my head, but I didn't dare make a move in case he came to his senses and decided that touching me was a bad thing. Because as far as my body was concerned, this was a very, *very* good thing. Dangerous, but good.

"Why did you run?" he asked, his eyes meeting mine.

"Wait...what? You're going to ignore what just happened?"

"Yes. Why did you run?"

I put my hands on his and removed them from my face, sitting back on the bench and looking away from him.

"The whole thing was embarrassing, Santi. It was like high school all over again, except this time, you were there to witness it."

"They did that to you in high school?"

I nodded.

"I was in the same class as Jenny's cousin. We were lab partners for a while. She wanted to study together, so I agreed because I needed good grades to get into college. I was never one of those really smart kids that got good grades easily, you know? I had to work hard for it, so I figured it wouldn't hurt doing extra. One time, when my parents were home, she said we should study in my room because they were distracting. I didn't question it because my mom always liked fussing over any friends I brought home because it was such a rare thing. My parents knew I was gay, but Christy didn't. As soon as we were in the room, she tried to kiss me, and I pushed her away. She laughed it off and left."

Even though it had happened so long ago, it still hurt thinking about it.

"What happened after?" Santi asked.

"Our teacher said I had to work on my own. I asked him why, and he said everyone was already paired up, which wasn't true. When I saw Christy in class, she looked at me with such hatred, and I knew she'd spoken to the teacher. After that, there were all kinds of rumors spread by her, Jenny, and their friends. I don't think anyone cared much about me, but they made a point to say stuff every time I was within earshot."

"I'm so sorry, Micah. I'm sorry they said those things and hurt you all those years ago. Girls like that will never change. They'll never be more than high school bullies."

I nodded.

"Thanks. I appreciate that, but they're not wrong. Their words don't get to me anymore. I was more embarrassed that they did it in front of you. You didn't have to do that, you know? Pretend that you were with me."

Santi put his hand on my chin, which forced me to look at him. "Do you think I'm the kind of man who'd pretend to be with someone for pity?"

"God, Santi, I'm sorry. I didn't mean to offend you. That was not what I—"

"Fuck it. Come here," Santi growled before he pressed his lips against mine.

All the internal sirens that had been going off were suddenly shut down. It seemed Santi's lips had the ability to turn them off. Who'd have known?

It took me a second to give in. Okay, half a second.

Santi's lips were soft but demanding, sucking me in until I opened my mouth to let his tongue explore. Hell, explore wasn't even the word.

Ravish. That's what he was doing. He was ravishing me.

I needed to stop this kiss because I was getting hard enough that it would be noticeable. Not just that, there were people around. Yes, the bench had offered privacy from prying ears, but we weren't sheltered by any means.

Santi chased my lips as if he didn't want the kiss to end.

"Fuck," he breathed out, his lips still so close to mine. He pulled back and stared into my eyes again. "Micah, I didn't do it out of pity. They gave me an excuse to do something I wanted to do from the moment I saw you on the grass by the river."

"What?" I whispered.

"Touch you. Micah, you are breathtaking, kind, and generous. Any man would be proud to be with you. Don't listen to their voices. They're wrong."

I understood the words coming out of his mouth, but I struggled with what he was saying.

"Any man...not you," I said. Hell, if it didn't kill me, it'd make me stronger.

He let out a burdened sigh. "You have no idea how much I'd want to be that man. But I can't, Micah. I'm dealing with some shit right now, and I don't want to end up hurting you."

"Your eyes," I said, reaching out to his face and rubbing my thumb over his temple.

He closed his eyes and nodded.

"Wanna talk about it? I'm a doctor, after all."

He smiled but shook his head. "If I ever feel the need to smell random people's butts, you'll be my first call."

I laughed. "Good."

"Would you give me a ride home?" he asked.

"Absolutely. One condition," I said.

"Name it."

"I need help moving something heavy in the barn, and I can't do it on my own."

"You got it."

We walked side-by-side to my car. I couldn't help noticing how Santi looked around at everything.

I had so many questions, but I didn't want to take it a step too far. Based on his earlier reaction, it was a sore topic, or at least something new he was still adjusting to.

As it was, I was thankful he hadn't picked up on Jenny's comments about me being a virgin. Or maybe he'd ignored them.

Admitting I'd been bullied at school was one thing. Admitting I was still a virgin at almost thirty was another altogether.

Despite the hotter-than-the-earth's-core kiss, Santi didn't want to start anything. He was dealing with his stuff, and I understood that.

We could still be friends, couldn't we?

I could make sure my growing feelings for him didn't get any bigger, couldn't I?

SANTI

If I'd wanted the old Santi back, then I guessed kissing Micah the way I'd just done proved he was still there.

What the fuck had I been thinking?

Of course there were no regrets because Santiago Torres never regretted anything that felt good, and fuck, kissing Micah had felt more than good.

The way he'd let me claim his mouth spoke of his inexperience, but the way his pupils made his green eyes darker and full of need told me he'd enjoyed it as much as I did.

And that was only one of the reasons I needed to not do it again.

I couldn't be one of the people that hurt Micah, and I knew I wasn't in the right headspace to get into a relationship with anyone.

One day, in the not-so-distant future, I'd be blind. It would start with little things like what happened earlier. Initially, I'd work around it, trying to pretend it wasn't happening until I couldn't pretend any longer.

Micah had his clinic and his animals. He was a busy

man. The last thing he needed was a disabled man dragging behind him.

I put my thoughts behind me as we arrived at the clinic.

For now, my eyesight was still good enough, and Micah needed help.

I followed him through the clinic and to the back of the house. This time, it only took me a moment to adjust to the change in lighting from briefly being indoors.

The backyard was segmented. The part closest to the house had a small decking with a couple of chairs and a grill. The rest was grass.

"Who are these guys?" I asked, pointing at two cats curled up together on one of the chairs.

"That's Salt and Pepper. They're Mindy's kids. Mindy is inside at the moment because she's close to having a new litter of kittens."

Micah gave both cats a good scratch, and then we went to the middle part of the garden, which had a wooden fence all the way around.

As we approached, I understood why. There were two dogs and three puppies playing with some toys. As soon as they saw Micah, they all started barking and jumping to get to him.

He opened the small gate to go inside and kneeled on the grass. The bigger dogs got closer to get some attention before letting the puppies have their time with Micah.

I took my phone out and snapped a photo before he could notice, and then bent over to scratch behind the floppy ears of the bigger dogs. They didn't look like they were a breed I recognized, so they were probably a mix.

Micah was talking to the puppies as if they could understand him. There was no shyness or uncertainty. Around the animals, he was relaxed and in control.

He called out each of the dogs' names, and they all sat in front of him.

"I'll give you a treat if you keep the noise down and you're nice to our guest, okay?" he said, holding one hand up while the other held a bag with something inside.

The dogs barked, and he gave them a look that meant business.

It was adorable to see the dogs desperately trying to contain their excitement as Micah placed a couple of treats in front of all of the dogs but one.

"Sheila has diabetes, so she knows she can't have these treats, but she gets extra cuddles and special food later," he explained.

As soon as he lowered his hand, the dogs went for the treats while Sheila ran to him and lay on her back for a tummy rub.

From the sounds she was making, it looked as though she preferred her personal attention to the food treats. I couldn't say I blamed her.

If Micah asked me to roll over and lie on my back, I'd do it in a heartbeat.

I snorted at my own thought.

"What?" he asked.

"You really don't want to know."

He stood and gestured for me to follow him through the gate on the other side.

I thought the garden ended with the tall hedge, but as we followed the opening at one end, I realized just how big Micah's property was.

"Wow, is this all yours?" I asked.

There was a chicken coop next to the hedge, which was surrounded by wire—probably to protect the chickens from being attacked by other animals—another enclosure that had a tiny goat in it, a large barn, and a field as that expanded as far as the eye could see.

"Yeah. This was my grandad's place. He always had his clinic up front. The rest of the land is just the field. I'll never do anything with it since it's good for wildlife."

"And you have a barn. If you have a stack of hay somewhere, I may have to make a few dirty jokes."

He laughed. "No hay, but something tells me you're the kind of guy who doesn't need props to make a dirty joke."

I winked and smiled as a pretty blush appeared on his light skin.

We went over to the barn.

"I was going to pull it down to build a sanctuary for the animals, but..." he trailed off, staring at the big building. "Anyway, I'm clearing it so I can move the dogs here in the winter. This spring was hard on them when we had a cold spell. I had to keep them upstairs at my place. That's not an experience I want to repeat."

He laughed, but I could tell this was something that worried him.

"How can I help?"

"This way."

He opened the large sliding doors to the barn, and I gasped when I saw the mess inside.

"I know. Grandad was a hoarder. I can't clear it all, but maybe I can make enough space. I've already taken so much stuff to the junkyard."

"Some of these would look great in your garden," I said, looking at an iron wheelbarrow and a bench.

"I know. I've got to prioritize now. It's not like I even have time to sit in the garden. Most days, I'm out here until it's dark. I really shouldn't be this fat, considering how many dinners I miss."

I knew he made the comment as a joke, but it brought back the stupid comments I'd overheard earlier, and I didn't like it.

Before I knew it, old Santi was back and had Micah pressed against the heavy door of the barn.

"Don't do that," I said against the skin of his neck. I liked feeling the goosebumps come up as my breath ghosted his skin. It meant he wasn't unaffected by me.

Maybe he'd listen better this way.

"Do what?"

"Talk about yourself that way. Micah, you are perfect. I like your roundness, your softness. My eyes haven't left your ass for a second since we got out of the car. Want to know a secret? I noticed you in high school too. I was just too confused by my feelings to understand why I got hard every time you walked past. Do you hear me?"

He nodded.

"As long as you're healthy and happy, you're perfect. You're not fat. You don't need to lose weight. You're fucking perfect, okay?"

Another nod.

"Good." I couldn't help leaning further into him. He felt so fucking good.

"Santi," he gasped. "Are you...hard?"

"For you, Micah Sawyer? Always."

He groaned, and I forced myself to take a step back from him. We were both breathless, and we hadn't even done anything. What would happen if I ever got under Micah?

Would stars collide? Whole solar systems form?

Nothing, because you're not going to find out.

I cursed my internal voice.

"Um...Santi?"

"Yes?"

"Jenny was right about one thing."

Micah's voice was laced with vulnerability. I was pretty sure Jenny hadn't been right about a single thing in her shallow little life.

"What was that?"

"I really am...um...I've never...I've never been with anyone."

I stared at him, my brain trying to remember what Jenny had said. What did he mean?

Oh.

"You're..."

He nodded. "It's not a big deal. I mean, I'm not in a cult or anything, like they said. I just...it never happened. I was busy with college and...you know you said I shouldn't say it, but the way I look has affected things. Guys at college never looked twice at me."

The more he spoke, the more I wanted to pull him into my arms and protect him for the rest of his life. I wanted Micah to be happy and never have an ounce of self-doubt.

I took a step forward and cradled his face with my hands. He was so goddamn beautiful.

"Thank you for telling me. I would never judge you or make fun of you, okay? I hope you still remember what I said earlier."

He nodded.

"Okay. Good. So, what is this thing that you need help moving?"

He blushed. "Um...yes...the um...wood."

I snorted.

He pointed to a pile of heavy-looking wood beams, and I laughed.

"Ahh, *that* wood. Got it."

We worked together, moving the beams one by one out of the barn.

"These would make amazing furniture," I said after we'd moved them all into a neat stack.

"Yeah, I think that's why Grandad got them. I have no idea what to do with them. I seriously lack in the handyman department."

I bit my lip to stop my mouth from running another joke. Old Santi needed to retreat for a moment.

"You haven't really gained much space by moving those beams. There's still all this other stuff."

"I know, but I can move the rest on my own. Thank you so much for your help, Santi."

"I'd like to help you," I said, already planning in my head a strategy to clear the space.

Micah laughed. "You already did enough today. Let me give you a ride home."

"I mean tomorrow or any other day. I have nothing to do, and I'm going out of my mind with boredom. Well, when I'm not going around the neighborhood returning stolen pets. Seriously, Micah. I'd love to help you. You already work hard enough as it is."

He stared at me for a moment. "One condition."

"Okay..."

"What happened at the bench and just now can't happen again."

He was right. It couldn't happen again.

"You have my word."

"Thank you. Okay, let me give you a ride."

I groaned. "Micah..."

His laugh rippled all the way down to my dick.

This was going to be a nightmare, but I knew there was no way I'd change my mind about helping Micah.

MICAH

"**W**ow."

"Jesus, Troy. Warn a guy," I said, bringing my hand to my chest.

"I could say the same. Why didn't you tell me you had eye candy? I'd have left the store in a heartbeat," he said, stretching up to get a better view of the garden.

"Isn't he a little too old for you?"

"What does that have to do with anything? I also lust after Matt Bomer, and he's old enough to be my dad."

I laughed. Troy had come over to visit the newborn kittens and had offered to clean out Mindy's crate and feed the animals but was clearly distracted by the same thing that had my attention.

Santi was shirtless in my backyard and playing with the dogs. Olive was with him. Even though she towered over all the other animals, she was a complete softie.

How was I supposed to focus on work when my kryptonite was right there within reach?

A hot man who could totally throw me around in bed

and also liked animals. How is a guy meant to resist? Especially after the things he'd said the other day?

I still couldn't believe Santi thought I was hot. Or that he'd kissed me once and almost a second time. Even my inexperience hadn't put him off if the bulge in his jeans was anything to go by.

"You know where the pet food is. Just don't get too distracted with Mr. Ripped-Abs and give Shirley the wrong food," I said to Troy.

"So you also think he's hot...hmm...I see..."

"You see...that I have eyes?" I punched him lightly on his arm and went back to the exam room to wait for my next patient.

Nothing good would come from lusting after Santi. He was only here to help, nothing else.

Fortunately, my patients provided enough distraction to last the rest of the day.

"Hi, April, ready to call it quits?" I asked my assistant as she was shutting her computer down for the day.

"Oh yeah, but I'm glad we've been busy, doctor. I'm spreading the word amongst friends about the pets. There's a few interested in the kittens, but it's harder to convince someone to take an older dog."

I let out a sigh, leaning against the reception desk.

"I know, and I appreciate you spreading the word. Can you lock the door after yourself? I'm heading out back to see if Santi needs a ride home."

"Will do, doc. Oh, maybe cook the man a nice dinner for his work. I hear he's single."

"April!"

She laughed and gave me a kiss on the cheek before grabbing her purse to go.

April had worked for an accountancy firm most of her

adult life. After retiring, she found herself bored, so as soon as she heard I was reopening the clinic, she'd knocked on the door asking for a job. Her pitch had included cake, so I'd hired her on the spot.

I took a deep breath before going back outside, seriously hoping Santi was no longer shirtless because there was a strong possibility I'd jump him and beg him to take my virginity, my money, and my sanity all in one go.

What would it be like to have sex with Santi?

He looked so strong but gentle. I bet he was a generous lover. Someone who'd make his partner feel wanted, sexy, and like they were the most important thing in the world. He would take his time. Nothing would be rushed with Santi.

My whole body erupted in goosebumps at the thought of being at Santi's mercy. Letting him touch me where no other man had ever touched before.

God, his kisses were incendiary. What would it be like to feel him inside me?

"Ugh, stop it."

"Stop what?"

I jumped as Santi came into the backroom from the room where Mindy was being kept with her kittens.

"Noth...nothing. Um, are you ready to go home? I mean...um, I can give you a ride, or maybe if you want something to eat, I'm sure I can—"

"Micah," he said with a gentle voice that traveled through my gut and straight to my cock. "Relax. You look like you're wound really tight. Busy day?"

"Yeah...busy."

"Want to see what I've done today?"

I nodded and followed him out. With the sun setting,

there wasn't as much contrast in lighting from inside to outside, so Santi walked out without any issues.

There was no way I'd tell him that I'd looked up his symptoms and had an idea of what might be wrong with his eyes. He could tell me himself when he was ready.

My heart broke for him if my suspicions were correct. He was the kind of man who got things done himself, the kind of man who'd grumble about his menagerie of pets but wouldn't have it any other way. He was fierce and independent.

How would he cope if he became blind? Because I could already tell from his dismissal when I tried to help him over my lunch break that he was also someone who liked to be in control and do things a certain way.

"I separated things into sections for you," Santi said. "All of this can go to the junkyard. It's either broken stuff or totally useless." He pointed at a pile of stuff outside the barn.

"Santi, this is... How did you do all of this on your own?"

He grinned and flexed his arm to show off his muscles.

"Impressive," I deadpanned, even though, given a chance, I'd lick his muscles, no questions asked.

"If you think this is impressive, you should see the rest of me."

"I've seen half of you, and so has Troy Mason, for that matter. Don't be surprised if you start getting fan mail and requests for photos and samples of chest hair."

"What hair?" he asked, lifting his shirt to give me a close-up view of his ridiculously defined abs.

"You should be illegal," I groaned.

"This is not even the impressive half of me," he teased.

I ran my hands over my face and took a deep breath. "Um...what else did you do?"

He pointed to a different pile of stuff. "These things are the interesting ones. I think you could repurpose some. Did you know you had a bathtub in there?"

"A bathtub? God, I loved my grandad, but I don't like him very much right now. What do I do with a bathtub? Shouldn't it go to the junkyard?"

"It could, but it's a beautiful antique tub, and you could use it as a planter for flowers or even vegetables."

I raised my eyebrows. Like I had time to look after flowers or vegetables.

"Do you know how easy it is to grow potatoes? And your garden has the perfect lighting for tomatoes and peppers," he said.

"How do you know all of that?"

His smile dropped, and I regretted asking the question immediately.

"I used to read a lot in my downtime," he said.

"Down time from what?"

He rubbed his chest as if reaching out for something that wasn't there.

"I was in the military. During downtime or between deployments, I spent my time reading and researching this stuff. I wanted to buy a piece of land one day, build a house and grow my own vegetables, fruit, that kind of thing."

I walked over and stood in front of him. "Why are you talking as if that's a past dream?"

His dark eyes met mine. "Because I can't have that anymore. Micah, I'm going blind. My condition took away my career and those dreams all in one go."

There were so many things I wanted to say to disagree

with him, but the way he looked at me, I knew he wasn't ready to hear it.

"Will you help me move the tub to the garden and pick something to plant in it?" I asked.

His smile was warm, and he ran his hand over my hair until it rested on my shoulder. "It would be my pleasure."

"Thank you. Just don't do it shirtless because I'm not sure I can take all that hotness so close to the house," I said.

He laughed. "Come on, let me show you the barn."

Once again, I was speechless at how much space Santi had freed up in just one day.

"Did you say you were going to tear it down to build a sanctuary for the animals?" he asked.

"Yeah, the contractors did a survey and said the barn wouldn't survive next winter."

"Bullshit. This barn is solid. You can use the structure and just add the stuff you need for the animals."

I shrugged. "Doesn't matter. They filed for bankruptcy, so I've lost my money. I can't tear the barn down or rebuild. Hell, I'm not even sure I'll have it in good enough condition to keep the dogs here over winter. I'm trying to spread the word out about fostering the dogs and the cats, but it's a challenge. Especially when we keep getting requests to take in more rescues."

"I'll help you. If you don't mind me bringing Duchess, Gus, and Alfie with me, I'll work here as long as it takes to make this ready."

"Why?"

He held up an old and rusty watering can. "Will you believe me if I tell you I need it? That I need to do this for me too?"

"I believe you."

"Hmm, Micah...baby..." His tongue ran through my lips, urging me to open up and taste him.

I was barely awake, but this was already the best wake-up call ever...until the smell...what the...

I opened my eyes to find myself staring at my dog.

"What the fuck, Pickles?" I groaned, sitting up on the bed and cleaning his slobber from my face.

I should have known even before I woke up that my dream was just a dream, but damn, it was so good.

We'd driven out to the coast and spent the day on the beach. Lazy kisses in the sun. Playing on the water until we were both hard and then slowing things down, knowing there would be more later.

He'd let me run my hands all over his body. I loved the roundness of his belly, the fullness of his ass. He'd told me how much he wanted me to fuck him.

Shame it was just a dream.

I groaned. The more time I spent with Micah, the more attracted I was to him.

He walked around talking to the animals, checking in on them between seeing his patients. He brought me water and snacks while I worked and constantly asked if I needed help.

Micah didn't know how magnetic he was. How every time he did something nice for me, it made me want to drag him into the barn and have my way with him.

It was only the knowledge that he'd never been with another man, and the promise I'd made, that stopped me from acting on my attraction. Because I knew Micah wasn't the kind of guy who did hookups. If he was, he wouldn't still be a virgin.

And I couldn't be the man he deserved. So I'd relegated my attraction to my dreams. In my dreams, I could touch him as much as I wanted, even if it always felt like it wasn't enough.

Noise coming from the bathroom caught my attention.

"Olive, is there anything I need to know about what's going on in there?" I asked the dog, even though I had my suspicions as to what was going on.

She howled at me, which evoked a quack from her partner in crime.

I reluctantly got out of the bed, already dreading going into the bathroom, even though I needed to pee.

"Gus, I'm coming in. There better not be a mess in there," I warned.

What I saw in the bathroom was definitely not what I thought I was going to see.

"How the fuck did I sleep through this?" I said to myself as I stared at Gus floating in a filled-up bathtub with Alfie fast asleep on top of him.

I had to hand it to them. If they didn't look so cute, I'd be shouting to get them out of my bathroom. Instead, I went back to the bedroom to grab my phone so I could snap a photo of the pair and send it to Micah.

If that wasn't proof I wasn't well in the head, I didn't know what was.

I picked up Alfie carefully and deposited him on my bed while I coaxed a reluctant Gus out of the bathtub. It was bad enough that Olive couldn't let me shower alone for fear that I'd drown. I drew the line at peeing with a full audience.

A quick shower later, I felt refreshed and ready to tackle the day...not that I had anything to do. Micah had specifically prohibited me from going to his place today.

Apparently, I'd become a little obsessed with clearing out his barn and was too efficient.

Sue a guy for wanting a job well done.

Totally nothing to do with craving being around him. At all.

I didn't even invite him to have dinner later as an excuse to see him today.

Nope.

Olive howled at me from the bathroom door.

"I know, I know. I don't believe my bullshit either."

I was filling my second cup with coffee when the doorbell rang.

As soon as I opened the door, I was surrounded by one hundred and ninety pounds of James Lexington-Bennett, who was now James Williams since he'd married his childhood best friend last spring.

"Man, stop squishing a dude. This is too gay, even for us," I joked.

He looked me up and down before seemingly satisfied that I was in one piece and then walked in, going straight to the kitchen.

"Is it cancer?" he asked.

"What?"

"Do you have cancer?"

Even though he was helping himself to my coffee, I could tell he was anything but relaxed.

"No, what makes you say that?"

"Ryan called. Why didn't you tell me you were back? You know I'm only around the corner in Windsor. I'd have come."

I waved my hand in front of him. "*This* is why I didn't call. You do realize I'm an adult, right?"

"An adult would appreciate that his kid brother and best friend are worried sick and feel helpless all the way across the world."

"Serves them right for moving all the way to Lydovia." I sighed. "Sit down before you have an aneurism."

There was no escaping him, and unlike my brother and Ryan, who only saw me on our video calls, James was right in front of me. It wouldn't take long for him to figure out what was wrong.

I sat in front of him and did my best to explain my condition to him.

"So...you can still see me," he said.

"Yeah, I still see, but I'm starting to get tunnel vision, and I struggle when going from dim to bright lighting and the other way round. I have night blindness, and sometimes my vision gets blurry. It'll get gradually worse, and no one can tell me how quick it'll happen."

He stared at me, and the pity I thought I'd see in his eyes wasn't there. There was concern, but not pity. That alone put a lump in my throat.

I needed to change the topic before I broke down and he thought I was depressed, or something. Knowing him, he'd kidnap me to his big estate in Windsor so he could keep an eye on me.

"Where's your husband? I'm surprised you got out of bed long enough to visit."

His face lit up at the mention of Connor.

"He's gone to the vet with Bubbles. She's been acting weird lately. Well...weirder. That turtle is fucking strange."

I snorted. "You want weird? Look at this." I took out my phone and showed him the photo I'd taken earlier.

"Where are they?"

"Knowing my luck, they're plotting something that means I'll need to go around the neighborhood apologizing to everyone...again."

As if they knew we were talking about them, Olive came in with Alfie on her back, followed by Gus.

James laughed. "Okay, you win on the weird pet front. Now you just need a guy to satisfy your other needs," he said, wiggling his brows.

"I'm not interested in hookups."

"Who said anything about hookups? You're here for good, right? You can date without the pressure of leaving someone behind and missing them. I know I could never have lasted in the military if I'd been with Connor while I was deployed."

I stood to open the backyard door for Olive. She wouldn't use the dog flap if she was carrying Alfie, and god forbid the kitten actually used his legs to move from one place to another.

"I'm fine on my own," I said.

James narrowed his eyes.

There was another knock on the door, and he stood. "That's Connor. I told him I'd be here."

"James...can we keep this between us?"

He stared at me with concern. I knew it was unfair to ask him to keep something from his husband, but I wasn't ready yet.

Maybe I was still trying to hold on to old Santi, but I needed to feel normal for as long as I could until I wasn't anymore.

He nodded.

I added more coffee and water to the machine and turned it on.

A moment later, James came back with Connor behind him.

They both sat at the table.

"Okay, you want the good or the bad news?" Connor said, looking at James.

"Is everything okay with Bubbles? Where is she?" James asked immediately.

"She's more than okay. The little devil went and got herself knocked up. We're soon-to-be grandads."

I snorted.

"What is the good news?" James asked, running his hands through his short hair.

Connor lit up and looked at both of us. "I bumped into Troy on my way to the vet. He was upset because, apparently, Micah has had this hot piece of hunk—Troy's words —working in the barn, but he wasn't there today."

James narrowed his eyes, and I bit my lip to keep myself from laughing.

"And this is good news because...?"

Connor rolled his eyes. "Babe, you remember how Micah was at school, right? Always on his own and very shy. If he's hooking up with the hot hunk, that's great news."

"Micah isn't hooking up with anyone," I said, leaning against the sink.

They both stared at me.

"How do you...? Oh my god," Connor said, raising his hand to his mouth and then pointing at me. "*You're* the hot hunk."

It was my turn to roll my eyes. "We're friends, and I'm helping him out because he was taken for a ride by the contractors he hired to build his animal sanctuary."

"Shirtless?" Connor asked.

"What?" James looked at me.

"Have you tried doing back-breaking work in this heat? I take my shirt off sometimes. Sue me."

They both sat back and crossed their arms, grinning at me.

"You can take those smiles off your faces. Or even better. You can fuck-off home because I need to get started on dinner. I'm doing a slow-roasted pulled pork for Micah and—" I stopped myself, realizing I wasn't helping things.

They laughed all the way out the door.

Fucking friends.

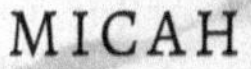

"Where are we going?" I looked at my watch. I was pretty sure I had a patient scheduled.

"We're going to the farmer's market," Santi said, pulling me by the hand toward my car.

"But—"

"The only butt I want to see is yours in the driver's seat. April has checked your schedule, and you can be away for a couple of hours."

"A couple of hours?" I couldn't be away for two hours. I had things to do.

Santi pushed me into the car, pressing his big body against mine.

"I kissed you to shut you up once; I'll break my promise, but I'll do it again. We're going to the farmer's market."

God. His voice when he spoke to me like that. Jesus Christ on a cracker.

"Okay," I agreed, trying my best not to sound all breathy and needy. "We'll go to the farmer's market."

He grinned as if he'd won a battle and then went around the car to the passenger side.

I had to wait three seconds to command my dick back down before I got in the driver's seat.

"See if you can find a parking spot close to the market," he said.

We hadn't spoken about his eyesight since that first day by the barn. He'd been working almost every day to clear it, and it already looked like an entirely different building.

I was actually glad the contractors hadn't done the job because, without all the junk inside, the building was perfect. It had power and water supply in the correct places and lots of potential. I just wished I hadn't lost the money because I could really use it now to finish off the sanctuary.

In the time Santi had been working, I hadn't noticed anything different about him, but I also knew he was stubborn and trying to ignore the inevitable changes coming to his life.

Was the request to park near the market because it was too bright out? After all, it was lunchtime and the sun was at its highest. There was also not a single cloud in the sky.

For the first time in my life, I wished for cloudy skies and anything else that would make it easier for Santi to see the world for as long as he could.

I couldn't remember the last time I'd been to the farmer's market in Chester Falls. Maybe even before I went to college.

"Look." He pointed at a stall that was full of flowers and trays with tiny green plants.

"Is that why we're here?"

Santi grinned. "Yes. I called ahead, and they're delivering the soil as we speak. All you have to do is decide if you want flowers or vegetables in your bathtub."

I stared at him. "What do you mean they're delivering the soil? Who? And who's—"

He put a finger over my lips. "Remember my earlier threat."

I nodded, but what if I wanted him to shut me up with a kiss?

"This is my gift to you, okay?" he said.

"But you're already doing so much, and I haven't paid you anything."

He tilted his head and narrowed his eyes. "You want a kiss, don't you? Is that why you're arguing with me?"

"I do want a kiss, but that's beside the—"

The bastard did shut me up. And continued to shut me up for a whole minute until someone coughing got our attention.

"Got the message?" he asked.

I swallowed, trying to calm down my racing heart. "Loud and clear."

"Good. So...flowers or vegetables?"

"Flowers? I'd love a vegetable patch, but I don't think I have time to tend to it at the moment. Besides, I have a whole field behind the barn. I can plant stuff there at some point."

He nodded. "Good point."

We spent some time looking at the flowers, but in the end, I picked a few lavender plants. They were good for the bees and would look really pretty on top of the bathtub.

The guy from the stall put the plants on a cart, and Santi pushed it to the car.

"Is this why you wanted to park close by?" I asked.

"Yeah, why did you think it was?"

"Nothing, no reason."

He returned the cart and then took me by the hand over to the burger stall. He ordered us burgers and drinks before leading me to an empty bench on the periphery of the square.

"Did you plan this all along?" I asked, taking a bite of my burger.

"I may have had a little help," he said.

"April." I shook my head. That woman needed to be reminded that matchmaking was not part of her job.

I finished my burger and wiped my hands with the napkin.

"Santi, I want to thank you for everything you're doing for me. The barn and now this," I gestured to the market and the flower stand. "I'm really sorry I can't pay you, but there must be something I can do for you."

"You've already done it," he said.

I pursed my lips. "How?"

"You're my friend. When I'm around you, and when I'm working at the barn, I don't feel like a disabled person, like I'm broken and beyond fixing."

He threw his napkin in a nearby trash can and then held my hands. "The military was everything for me all of my adult life. I'm on borrowed time now. Doing this stuff for you is the only opportunity I'll ever have to feel normal before it all ends."

I got it, but I didn't accept it. He wasn't broken. His life would change, but it wouldn't be over. He was talking like he was as good as dead the moment he lost his eyesight.

"Santi. If there was something you could do before you lose your eyesight, what would it be?"

He broke eye contact. "I...I haven't thought about it."

I put my hand on his chin to make him look at me. "Tell me..."

He smiled. "I think I'd like to go to the beach. I've spent

the last twelve years in the desert. I'd love to swim in the ocean and look at the horizon."

"We can go to the beach on my next day off...if you want, that is."

"I want to kiss you so much right now, Micah Sawyer," he said, rubbing his thumbs over the palms of my hands.

"Maybe later," I said.

He smiled. "Maybe later."

"Micah! Oh my vanilla-cupcakes-with-double-frosting-and-sprinkles, I'm so glad to see you."

I laughed at Tom's over-the-top greeting.

"Hi, Tom."

He gave me a hug and only seemed to notice Santi when he stood back.

"And who's this piece of man hunk? Micah, you're a little unicorn, aren't you? Full of surprises."

Santi looked a little scared.

"Tom, this is Santiago Torres. He moved back to Chester Falls recently. Santi, this is Tom. He owns that fashion store over there," I said, pointing to Fabulize.

"There are so many things I want to say that my brain is about to explode like a glitter bomb, so listen to me, Micah. I have a solution for your problem," Tom said, jumping from foot to foot as if he really were about to explode.

"My problem?"

"I've been thinking about how the town can help you raise money for the sanctuary. I spoke to some friends, and everyone agrees that it should be a town effort. After all, you're taking care of animals that no one wants. You're practically a saint."

I laughed. "Tom, I'm far from being a saint," I said, hitting Santi when he snorted.

"Bachelor auction," Tom said.

"I'm sorry?"

"I've already spoken to Connor, and they're happy to host the event at Lexington-Bennett Hall." Tom raised his hands as if he were holding a banner. "Glitz and glamor. Think the Met Gala is fashionable? It'll be nothing compared to our fundraiser. All the invited eligible bachelors will be auctioned for a date, and the proceeds will go to help you build and run the sanctuary."

"Tom, that's—"

"Glitzingly perfect, right? Don't worry, leave it to me. I've got it all planned." And then he turned around and walked back toward his store.

"I'm scared to ask what that was," Santi said.

"That is probably one of the kindest, funniest, sparkliest people you'll ever meet...as long as you're not at the other end of one of his fabulous plans."

"Was he serious? About the fundraiser?"

I shrugged. "With Tom, anything is possible. Do you think it will work?"

"Who knows. But I do think you deserve to have the support of the town. Tom is right; the work you do is for the good of everyone. You keep the strays and give them a home when no one else wants them. I think you might be related to Pickles."

I laughed aloud.

"You know if this thing happens, you're getting an invite, right?" I asked.

"I'm counting on it."

"You also realize Tom will make sure you're one of the bachelors on auction."

"Shit."

Santi's panicked face made me laugh even harder. I wouldn't doubt that in an auction situation, there would be a bidding war for the chance to spend some time with him.

Who wouldn't want to? He was funny and sexy as hell.

I tried not to think of our kiss earlier and the promise of more. There was no doubt I wanted more, but I shouldn't.

Santi was as addictive as ice cream. One scoop was never enough. Summer or winter, it didn't matter. I still wanted ice cream, regardless of the weather. I was starting to think the same about him.

"We should get back," I said, standing up. "I have a couple of surgeries booked for this afternoon. It's going to be pretty busy.

"Oh, okay. Let's go."

My patients kept me busy the rest of the afternoon, which was exactly the kind of distraction I needed. By the time I finished my last surgery and checked in on all the animals, Santi had left.

The apartment upstairs from the clinic felt too quiet, and for once, I was at a loss for how to spend my evening.

I took a quick shower and then headed to the kitchen, thinking about what to have for dinner. My phone buzzed with a message.

Santi: Sorry I missed you earlier. Olive kept pestering me to go home to Alfie.

I smiled at the screen, imagining an excited Olive pulling on Santi's shirt to get home to see her friend.

· · ·

Micah: You gotta keep the girl happy. Thank you for the planter and the flowers. They look amazing.

I started typing a reply when Santi's name appeared on the screen.

"Hello," I said into the phone.

"Hey."

"Everything okay? I was just replying."

"Um...yeah. I was wondering..." He paused for a moment. "Did you mean what you said earlier?"

I tried to think about what we talked about.

"Which part?"

"Going to the beach."

It was a good thing we were on the phone because there was no way to disguise the smile on my face.

"Of course. This Sunday?" I asked.

"Sounds great. Thank you, Micah."

I wanted to say I was the one who needed to thank him, but I already knew he'd shrug it off.

"Pick you up at ten?"

"Perfect."

SANTI

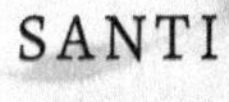

I sat outside the house on the porch steps and looked at my watch. Half-past nine.

Micah said he'd be here at ten, but the idea of going to the beach had me so excited that I'd been up since six and had already gone for a run, taken a shower, eaten breakfast, and I was still early.

I'd even dropped the spare key with my neighbor. She didn't mind checking in on Olive and Alfie, filling their water bowls, and giving them food while I was out.

I checked my small backpack for the hundredth time to make sure I didn't forget my sunglasses, water bottle, and wallet. Micah hadn't mentioned taking food with us, so I assumed we'd find somewhere to eat on the beach.

Why did I feel like a teenager waiting for his date to arrive?

Watching Micah laugh at my expense after Tom had left us was the best thing in the world.

Because, yeah, entering a bachelor auction was as low on my bucket list as eating snails. As in, it wasn't there at all.

Unlike making Micah smile. That was in the number one spot.

We'd returned back to the clinic in time for Micah to disappear into his consultation room to see his next patient, so I'd gone straight to the barn.

Pickles had been asleep next to her water bowl, which meant she'd been chasing rabbits out in the field all morning and had exhausted herself.

Micah had taken in another dog, which a family had brought in because their newborn baby was allergic. Gus seemed to have taken the dog under his literal wing and had even refused to come home for the last two days.

It wasn't a problem as long as I was still working in the barn, but he'd need to come home with me at some point. I couldn't leave Micah with another animal to look after.

I needed to shift my thinking when it came to Micah. His busy schedule had left us with few chances to spend time together in the last couple of days since the market.

Maybe time apart was what I needed to reset my brain and start thinking of Micah as just a friend and not someone I wanted to know better without clothes on.

Fifteen minutes later—I knew this because I checked my watch again—I saw Micah's car approach. I stood as he parked and came out of the car, walking toward me.

"Hey, are you ready?" he asked, smiling wide and looking as excited as I felt.

"Been ready for hours. I apologize in advance if I behave like a three-year-old trying candy for the first time."

He laughed. "Let's get going then."

As expected on a warm summer day, West Point Beach on the Long Island sound was packed with people. And as if he could tell the crowds made me a little uneasy, Micah came around the car to my side.

"Trust me?" he asked.

I nodded and followed as Micah grabbed a bag with beach towels from the trunk and then walked in the opposite direction from where the crowds were.

"Where are we going?"

"Further down this way, there's a private beach for residents only. A college friend lives there and said we could use it."

I didn't like that my first thought was wondering what kind of relationship Micah had with this friend that we were allowed on their private beach. But I pushed the thought aside and followed him.

Once we were through the expanse of sea grass dividing the residential area and the beach, I had to stop to take in the view.

Soft sand was kissed by small waves of clear water that expanded as far as I could see, with Long Island in the distance.

It wasn't the ocean, but it was fucking perfect as far as I was concerned. When I'd been deployed, I'd dreamed of going to the beach and staring at the water for hours. Those childhood memories of making new friends on vacation and playing with my brother making sand castles got me through many nights in the desert.

"Come on, let's get your feet wet. You know you want to," Micah said. I hadn't even noticed him laying the towels on the sand or how he'd removed his shirt and was now only in his swim trunks.

Micah had strong, thick thighs, and just as I'd imagined, a round belly that looked soft and just big enough to cuddle without being in the way. His skin was pale, which made the blond hairs on his chest stand out perfectly.

My fingers twitched with the need to touch him.

I looked away and removed my shirt before he noticed me staring at him with thoughts that were as far from platonic as my chance of recovering my twenty-twenty vision.

"Yeah, let's go," I said.

The water was cold, but nothing short of turning me into an ice cube would have stopped me from diving in.

"You're insane," Micah shouted from the water's edge, where he stood with his arms across his middle as if he were trying to cover himself up.

I walked out of the water slowly, not stopping until I was so close he had to tilt his head to look me in the eye.

Droplets from my hair fell on him, and I didn't miss the bobbing of his Adam's apple.

Before he could say anything or run, I bent down, picked him up in a fireman's lift, and ran back to the water, dropping him before diving under.

We both came up breathless and laughing.

"You fucking fucker," Micah shouted, placing his hands on my shoulders and making me go under again. "This water is freezing cold. I wouldn't even feel my nuts if they floated away."

I laughed. "That would be a real shame."

He splashed me, and I went for it again, diving under and lifting him.

"Let me down," he screamed.

"What? Now that I have you at my mercy? No chance," I teased.

Before he had a chance to reply, I threw him in the water. He came up looking like an advertisement for men's beachwear. Tousled hair, shiny green eyes, plump and kiss-able lips.

Was it me, or had the water warmed up by a few

degrees? I dove under the small waves to get away from Micah, begging my dick to calm down.

He shook his head at me before walking back to shore.

Once it was safe that I wouldn't walk out with a tent in my shorts, I joined him on the towel he laid next to his.

The sun was warm on my cool, wet skin. I lay on my belly and closed my eyes, listening to the sound of kids playing on the public beach in the far distance.

While there were some people around us, there were definitely not as many.

The lull of the waves on the beach was enough to send me to sleep. I didn't even notice until I woke up.

I turned my head to face Micah, who sat on his towel with his shirt back on. He had his legs crossed and was flipping his phone in his hands absentmindedly.

I followed his line of sight, hoping to find out what he seemed so distracted with.

There was a group of people a few yards away. A few of them were in couples and there were three kids playing in the sand.

Micah hadn't noticed I was awake, so I took my time admiring him before trying to figure out why he was staring at the group, looking like he wanted to be there.

Did he know them? Maybe he did. After all, he said his friend lived here. Maybe that was his friend's group, and he wanted to join them but couldn't because of me.

The thought made my stomach sink, and all the happiness from messing around earlier was gone.

"You can join them if you want," I said with more bite than he deserved. "I'm not a child. I'm more than capable of looking after myself."

Micah turned to me with a confused expression.

"Huh?"

"It's fine. Go ahead and hang out with your friends. I'll stay here. I won't even go in the water unsupervised." I sat up and turned around on the towel to face away from him. The last thing I needed was his pity, or to see him having fun with his friends.

Okay, that was an overreaction, but I couldn't help it. I wanted Micah for myself and couldn't have him.

The unmistakable sound of sand shifting as he walked away from me made me so angry. I wanted to chase him and tell him not to go, but I'd be damned if I was going to do that.

I was still stewing in my own anger when what felt like a gallon of cold water was dropped on my head.

"What the fuck," I shouted, turning around. My eyes looked for the culprit, stopping when they met Micah's angry gaze. "What did you do that for?"

"Because you were an asshole, and assholes get cold showers."

I stood to shake the towel that was now caked with wet sand.

"How was I an asshole?"

"I know we haven't been friends long, but have I ever treated you like you're any less? Have I ever given you the impression that I don't want to hang out with you?"

I opened my mouth and closed it again.

"I'm sorry, Micah. Fuck, I don't know what went through my head. You were staring at them..." I trailed off, knowing there was nothing I could say that could excuse my behavior.

"I don't even know who they are. I was looking because...it doesn't matter."

I sighed. How had I ruined what had been so far the most perfect day?

"Can I buy you lunch?" I asked.

"Is it an apology lunch?"

I stared at him, and a small smile grazed his lips.

"What's the difference?"

"If my friend is taking me to lunch, I want crab rolls. If my friend is apologizing for being an ass, then there's a restaurant that does amazing grilled steak about a mile from here."

I laughed. "What if this friend wants to apologize for being jealous because he wants you all to himself?"

His smile left his lips again, and he frowned, pulling his shirt down and pointing at the beach hut selling crab rolls and sandwiches. "Let's just get a snack."

"Okay."

There was a seating area on a raised deck right next to the beach hut, so I paid for our food and picked a table that had a parasol that offered some shade.

"Did you always want to be a vet?" I asked, hoping to get us back to how things were earlier.

"Yeah. Ever since I watched my grandad save a cat's life. He didn't even know I was watching him through the window."

"How old were you?"

"Eight. At first, I kept watching because there was so much blood. I couldn't see very well from a distance. After the surgery, he took the cat to the recovery room. Later that night, I sneaked out from his apartment upstairs. As soon as the cat saw me, he meowed. He couldn't move because of his bandages, but it was as if he were telling me my grandad had saved his life. I ran upstairs to my room, and that's when I decided I wanted to be a vet just like him."

I finished my drink and wiped the flour from the crab roll off of my hands.

"You do an amazing job, Micah. Your life...it has a purpose. You do good things."

There was a small blush crawling up from under his shirt, and just like earlier, I wanted nothing more than to touch him.

He stared at me as if he wanted to say something. I waited, but nothing came, and then he looked away.

"Wanna go back to the beach and get lobstered?" I asked, hitting his knee with mine under the table.

"Sounds like a bad life choice," he said with a chuckle.

"Meh, you only live once."

We stayed at the beach a few more hours before the increasing wind made it uncomfortable to stay longer, so Micah drove us back.

There was no way to explain to him how important this day at the beach had been to me, so I simply thanked him again when he dropped me off.

I'd see him at his place tomorrow to continue the work on his barn. This was the only way I knew to repay him for everything he'd done. Being my friend, taking me to the beach, and treating me like a full person rather than the half-person I felt like. Even when I was a dick.

My neighbor came out of her house when she saw me walk up the stairs and threw the spare keys at me.

"Oops," I said, failing to grab the keys before they landed on the floor next to my feet. "Believe it or not, I was never this clumsy in the army."

She laughed and waved me off. "Olive has been quiet today. Maybe she's finally growing out of her puppy stage."

I waved back and walked inside, feeling the mortification of not being able to catch a small set of keys from such an easy distance.

As soon as I was through the door, Alfie jumped on me, his claws digging painfully into my chest.

"Fuck, Alfie. What's wrong with you?"

He meowed and jumped on the floor as if telling me to follow him.

I locked the door and set both sets of keys on a side table before heading to the kitchen. I'd need to check with my neighbor when she'd last fed Alfie and Olive. I wouldn't put it past them to pretend they were starving to death in order to get more food.

Olive was on the tiled floor, which was unusual for her since she loved her bed, especially when Alfie was with her.

"What's the matter, girl?" I said gently, running my hand over her fur. Her stomach felt hard, almost like a balloon. That wasn't normal. Had she eaten something that made her ill?

I grabbed my phone and called a local cab company, keeping my voice as steady as I could as I asked for a ride to Micah's place.

Please, let this not be a serious thing. My poor girl.

MICAH

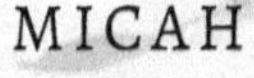

After dropping Santi off at his house, I decided to drive around for a while to get my thoughts in the right place.

Despite everything, today had been a great day. I just wished it hadn't left me feeling so confused.

Watching Santi's expression of childhood-like happiness as he stared at the water for the first time in years melted my heart. The way he'd jumped in, not caring about the temperature, and even when he effortlessly picked me up and dropped me in the water.

It was a good thing the water had been freezing because I would have really embarrassed myself if I'd gotten hard.

Santi was gorgeous, fun, and basically everything I wasn't. There were no two ways about it, and it didn't go unnoticed. From the girls that inched their way closer to us to the guy that had walked past a number of times, it seemed Santi drew everyone in with his looks alone.

I'd wanted to shout and tell them they didn't know the real Santi and to fuck off and leave us alone.

But while I'd drooled at the sight of the taught muscles

on his chest and abs, the way he'd looked at me after I'd taken my shirt off had me confused. Because unlike the time at the school or when we went out to the market, I didn't see the same hunger in his eyes when he looked at me.

All the insecurities I felt about my body came to the surface. Maybe it was one thing thinking I was attractive when my clothes hid all the ugly parts of my body. It was another altogether to be faced with the reality. That I wasn't a tall, slim, muscled guy like many of the guys he'd been with probably were.

Santi was all ripped muscles and tanned skin while I was round, flabby, and pasty-white.

But then...I couldn't explain his behavior. He'd more or less admitted to being jealous at the thought of me wanting to join the group of strangers on the beach.

Why would he be jealous? I thought that after the few kisses we'd had, he knew he could take anything from me, and I'd give it gladly. Didn't he know that?

Maybe he just didn't want me and those kisses had been a fluke.

"Why does this have to be so confusing and complicated?" I asked myself aloud, even though I didn't want to face the reply to that particular question.

And then there was the question I'd been considering asking Santi ever since the day at the market. I just hadn't found the courage to do it, and after today, I wasn't sure I ever would.

I took a deep breath and made my way home. April had come over earlier to feed the animals, so I had nothing left to do. Maybe I could use the rest of the day to prepare some healthy meals for the week.

I'd never be a runway model, but it couldn't hurt to lose

a few pounds. Maybe then I'd feel a little more confident about joining a dating app.

I ignored the thoughts in the back of my mind about not wanting anyone else but Santi or the stupid idea that he should be my first. Those thoughts weren't helpful or realistic.

As I turned the corner to my street, I noticed a large figure on the steps to the house.

Santi?

I parked in my spot and watched as he all but ran to me. His eyes were red, and his hair was all over the place.

"Santi, what are you doing here?"

"Micah, I need help. Olive...she's not well."

I went around the car, not worrying about taking the bag with the beach towels from the trunk.

"What happened?"

Santi didn't need to answer the question because as soon as I saw Olive on the porch steps, I knew what was wrong with her, and if I wasn't quick, she might not make it.

Alfie was right next to her, meowing as if he knew there was something very wrong with his best friend. He wasn't wrong.

"I don't know. She was on the floor when I got home. Maybe she swallowed something? Her belly isn't right."

I unlocked the front door and went straight to the examination room to grab the stretcher. I needed to minimize how much she was moved because I didn't know how long she'd been this way.

"Help me get her on the stretcher," I said. Santi put his hands on her hips, and I took the shoulders. "On three... one...two...three."

We moved her carefully onto the stretcher and then brought her into the examination room.

"I need to do an X-ray on her. Let's put her on that table."

Santi followed my instruction, talking gently to Olive as I turned the X-ray machine on and waited for the computer attached to boot up.

"She looks like she's in so much pain, Micah," he said.

"I know, I know," I said, using the touch screen on the machine. I didn't know what else to tell him.

I couldn't say she'd be okay soon because there was a high chance she wouldn't be, and right now, I needed to focus on Olive. As soon as she was stable, I could explain it all to Santi.

"Come on, we need to go to the other room for the X-ray. Let's put Alfie outside with Salt and Pepper."

His eyes were full of pain. He didn't want to leave Olive on her own.

"Hey," I said, cradling his face, making him focus on me. "This is what I do, okay?"

He nodded and then followed me out.

Alfie complained about being taken outside, but as soon as he saw the other cats, he curled up with them on the cushioned seats of my outdoor furniture.

The X-ray machine had been an expensive but much-needed addition to my practice, and now, more than any other time, I was so thankful for being able to diagnose the problem so easily.

We went back to the room as soon as I had all the X-rays that I needed.

I felt Santi's eyes on me, waiting to find out the diagno-sis, which was as I'd originally thought.

"She has Gastric Dilatation-Volvulus Syndrome, more

commonly known as gastric torsion. It's quite frequent in big dogs, and it means the stomach twists in on itself, which affects the blood supply," I explained as I grabbed everything I needed to relieve Olive of the buildup of gas and liquid in her stomach.

"What are you going to do?" he asked. "What caused it?"

"It's most likely inherited from her parents. This is quite common in Great Danes. Breeders should avoid breeding dogs with the condition so it doesn't get passed on, but often money speaks louder, and they don't care."

I didn't know if this was the case for Olive or if the girl had simply been too excited eating her food that she'd caused the problem herself. But I definitely didn't want Santi to feel guilty for being away for the day and leaving Olive in the care of someone else.

There was really a fifty-fifty chance of either thing causing the torsion in her stomach.

I put my hand on his arm, and he looked at me.

"You're tense and upset. She'll feel your stress, which could put her at a higher risk. I think you should go outside and wait, okay? I promise to take good care of her."

He nodded. "Will you call me back in when...if...?"

"I promise."

He left through the back door to the garden, and I turned to Olive.

"Okay, baby girl, it's you and me now."

I administered some pain relief so I could carry out the gastric decompression by inserting a needle into her side. Once I relieved her stomach from the excess gas, I could assess the next steps.

It was likely she'd need a gastropexy to stop the problem from occurring again, but it was a high-risk operation.

I thought of Santi outside and how helpless he'd

looked. I wanted to comfort him and tell him everything would be okay with Olive, but there was only one person who could make sure she really would be okay, and that was me.

As soon as I had her stable and pain-free, I could go back to the man outside and take his pain away.

Olive did great throughout. Her vitals were strong, which gave me confidence in the diagnosis and treatment. She wasn't completely out of the woods, but I was hopeful that she'd be one of the success cases.

I put her on a course of fluids as soon as I was able to draw some blood for analysis. That would help the success of the surgery tomorrow.

"Well done, baby girl. I'm so proud of you, and your daddy will be too, as soon as I tell him how great you did," I said, running my hand over her head and scratching her ears.

She didn't react other than to look at me. I knew she was exhausted from the ordeal and needed to sleep. I took her to the recovery room and set up the doggy cam connected to my phone before leaving her to rest.

I couldn't see Santi from the window, so I cleaned up the room and created a file for Olive on my computer. The admin was a calming exercise I always did after every procedure.

Leaning back in my chair, I took a deep breath.

Messing around on the beach. Crab rolls. Santi's blissful face staring at the water. It all felt like a million years ago.

I stood and went out to find him.

One thing I knew for sure about today, I wasn't going to leave Santi on his own to deal with this alone.

The T-shirt and shorts I'd worn to the beach were drenched in sweat, but I didn't care. I needed to keep moving, doing more, stretching my muscles to the point of pain.

I didn't want to think about Olive suffering inside the big house. And I definitely didn't want to consider that one of the ways her pain would stop was if she...no...I couldn't think like that.

Micah had been right to tell me to leave the room because I wouldn't have remained calm. As soon as I'd left the house, I'd been on a one-man mission to keep as busy as possible so I wouldn't count the minutes until there was any kind of news.

All the animals seemed to have been fed, so I checked their water bowls then cleaned the chicken coop. When that was done, I went inside the barn and started fixing some of the broken wooden slats.

At the rate I was going, Micah would have the barn ready by the end of the day. At least this was useful work. Despite his grandad hoarding a lot of useless stuff, he also had a good collection of tools that I was able to clean up and use.

The spare wood was good for the dog houses, which I was already planning on working on next.

"Santi, are you here?"

"Fuck," I shouted when the nail slipped and I hit my fingers with the hammer. I'd been so lost in my thoughts, I hadn't even heard Micah.

"Up here, coming down," I said. *Fuck, that hurt.*

I climbed down the ladder from the hayloft.

"Did you know you have actual hay up there?" I asked when I jumped off the last steps.

"Um...no? Santi..."

"I can install some lights for you up there. Take up some warm blankets, and it will be the perfect make-out location."

"Santi."

I was avoiding eye contact with Micah as much as I could because I couldn't bear to hear the news he had for me.

"I volunteer as tribute if you want to test it out." I looked down at my wet clothes. "I should probably shower first though."

"She's okay."

"What?" This time I looked at him.

He smiled and came closer. "I know what you're doing, Santi. She's okay. She's stable. I decompressed the gas and liquid from her stomach and did a small procedure to put it back in place. Her vitals were great throughout, and she's now on fluids. I took a blood sample, which I will test in the morning, as well as a new sample to make sure she doesn't have high sodium levels. If she doesn't, then I'll perform a surgery which is a little complex, but if it's successful, this won't happen again."

I stared at him as he explained everything. I didn't understand half of it, but I got the important stuff. She was okay. Olive was okay. And if she survived the surgery tomorrow, she'd continue to be okay.

"Micah," I said, my voice strained. "Thank—"

He put his hand over my mouth.

"Do not thank me, Santi." He started to say something but then narrowed his eyes and pursed his lips. "Actually, you can thank me by taking a shower. You stink."

I smiled under his hand and then wrapped my arms around him, lifting him off the floor.

"Ew, get off me and put me down."

"Or what?" I teased.

"Or I'll knee you in the balls."

I gasped. "You wouldn't."

"You're right. I'll probably die from your stench before I have a chance to hurt you."

I laughed and put him down.

He looked around at the walls where the previously broken slats were now fixed, keeping the barn insulated from the cold and rain.

"I still need to do the other wall, but it's mostly done. I can't believe the contractors wanted to pull this down. The barn is solid, especially with those cracks all fixed."

"Thank—"

I interrupted him by placing my hand over his mouth and giving him a look that meant business.

He chuckled and nodded.

"Okay, okay, how about you have a shower, and then I'll take you to visit Olive," he said.

We went back into the house through the staff area and

up the stairs to his apartment, where he showed me the bathroom attached to the guest room.

"I'll see if I have something that'll fit you while we put your clothes through the wash."

"Thanks. I really got carried away with work," I said, looking down at my sweaty and dirt-stained clothes.

"It's understandable. Although, in the same place, I'd have eaten my weight in ice cream instead."

He left the room, so I removed my clothes, put them in a pile on the bathroom floor, and turned the water on.

I looked in the mirror. My hair was all over the place, and I had a few scratches on my face.

When the hell did that happen?

After cleaning the day away in Micah's shower, I wrapped a towel around my hips and walked out. He'd laid a pair of shorts and a T-shirt on the bed.

I laughed when I put the shorts on. They were too short and a little tight. The shirt, which had a picture of a cute dog, was also short enough that I was showing skin.

"Is this your idea of a joke?" I asked, walking into the kitchen, where Micah was on his laptop. His hair was damp, so he must have had a shower at the same time as me.

My dick twitched at the thought of a naked Micah just across the hall from me, but fortunately, there wasn't much room to move in his tiny shorts.

He snorted, covering his mouth before falling into a fit of laughter.

"I'm glad I'm amusing you. You better get these washed if you ever want to get rid of me because I'm not leaving your place wearing these clothes." I threw my dirty clothes at him, which he narrowly missed by getting up too quick for me.

Olive was asleep when we went down to see her. Micah

checked her again and reassured me she was doing well and wasn't in pain. She'd also received the fluids well.

I was relieved enough to eat the piece of toast Micah put in front of me after we went back upstairs. The cup of coffee also helped settle my stomach, but I couldn't shake off the helplessness of seeing Olive so sick.

After washing the two dishes and coffee cups, we settled on Micah's couch.

"Do you want to watch something?" he asked. "I don't even know what's good on TV these days, but there must be a movie on one of the channels. It'll help distract you."

I shook my head. "I hated seeing her like that and not being able to do anything," I said. "I know I complain about the bruises on my legs because her tail is fierce, or when she brings other people's pets home with her, but she's my..." I trailed off. How could I explain what Olive meant to me?

"I understand," Micah said. He sat back on the couch and stared at the space in front of him. "She's your partner, your eyes, your instinct, your everything."

My words were trapped in my throat. Once again, Micah Sawyer, the shy kid I used to admire from afar in high school turned veterinarian doctor, got it.

"How do you do that?" I asked.

He looked at me with those big green eyes. I'd never noticed all the freckles under his eyes and over his nose. They must have come out due to sitting in the sun earlier.

"I spent twelve years cheating death, training soldiers, showing only what I wanted everyone to see. In only a few weeks, you have me decoded, Micah. How do you do it?"

He shrugged. "I don't know. Maybe..."

He moved his eyes so they were fixed on the dog picture on my shirt.

I placed a finger under his chin, raising his head so he

looked at me again. Those beautiful, honest, pure green eyes needed to be on me.

"Tell me..." I whispered.

"Santi, we couldn't be more different on the outside, but...sometimes I wonder if we're not more similar than we think on the inside. That's all."

"That's all?"

He nodded slowly, his gaze moving down to my mouth. His lips parted slightly, and I felt a little puff of air escape them.

Were we that close? When did that happen?

"Santi..."

His whisper was a prayer, a wish, but I couldn't do anything.

For the first time in my life, I was too scared to make a move on a man.

It seems I didn't need to because Micah narrowed the space between us and pressed his lips against mine.

It was one simple kiss, two sets of lips joined for a split moment before he pulled back and looked at me. His pupils were so dark, his eyes almost lost their usual color.

"More," I groaned and placed my hand behind his neck, pulling him closer. This time, he didn't stop at the one kiss. Even though he hadn't made a move to taste me, he also hadn't stopped kissing me.

It was driving me crazy, and my dick was begging me for some space in Micah's ridiculous shorts.

It was worse because I was turned sideways, but that was resolved quickly. With one move, I had Micah straddling me on the couch.

The way he was moaning into my lips, I wasn't even sure he noticed the change of position. He'd wrapped his arms over my shoulders and his hands gripped my hair tight.

I was sure to burst within the next minute if he kept at it, and how ridiculous was that?

In the past, I'd been able to last all night, drawing three, sometimes four orgasms from my partners, always coming hard but last.

With Micah, all that meant nothing. Because in the same way he understood me, he was also able to command my body.

"Jesus, Micah." I nipped and sucked the soft skin of his neck. His beard abrading my skin so good. "Fuck."

MICAH

Ohmygod, ohmygod, ohmygod.

My head was about to blow. Both of them.

Was this really happening?

What had started as a gesture to comfort Santi had become the single hottest thing I'd done in my entire life. And I still had clothes on.

In the same way that he'd effortlessly picked me up to throw me in the water, Santi had pulled me onto his lap, and I hadn't been able to stop it or resist.

My body was begging for Santi. Whatever he wanted to do to me was more than okay, as long as it ended with an orgasm. I was already so close, and we'd hardly done more than light kissing.

This felt different from the other times we'd kissed.

Before, it was about him teaching me a lesson. Telling me to stop listening to the voices in my head or of my past.

It was his way to give in to our attraction without giving or taking too much.

But now...now we were of equal standing.

He was as vulnerable as I was but for different reasons.

That thought made me feel powerful. Confident.

Whether that was right or wrong, I didn't know, but for the first time in my life, I wanted to be a normal man. Someone who a guy like Santi wanted so badly that he couldn't even think straight.

The way Santi's hands held on to my waist showed me that, today, I was that guy. I'd be damned if I was going to let any of my hang-ups get in the way.

I gripped his hair tight to keep him right where he was. I needed more of his soft, addicting lips.

Was kissing another person always like this?

"God, Micah, you're gorgeous," he rasped into my lips. "Let me taste you."

I opened up for him, shivering with anticipation, but unlike the first time, Santi didn't ravish me.

He savored me.

His tongue traced the outline of my lips before he sucked them into his mouth. Just when I thought I'd die from needing more, he closed his mouth over mine and took everything he wanted.

I was so hard it would have been impossible to hide it, not that I wanted to, quite the opposite. I wanted to show Santi what he was doing to me.

My hips moved against his, and I felt his erection.

Fuck, how big is he?

My hole twitched as I thought of Santi filling me and making me feel good.

"Santi," I whispered against his lips before kissing him some more.

"What do you need, Micah?"

"Hmm..."

He chuckled. "You're going to need to stop kissing me and use your words."

"No...your lips are too good. Can't stop."

His hands snaked around my back and down to cup my ass. He pressed his long fingers over my shorts against my hole, and I nearly jumped at how good it felt.

He pulled me harder against his erection, and I had to pull away from his kiss because I needed to breathe. Everything was too good, too sensitive.

I was overwhelmed in the best of ways but still not close enough to that blissful goal.

"Can I touch you, Micah?" he asked, sucking on my neck.

"Yes...mark me, please, Santi...mark me."

Another chuckle. "That's not what I meant."

"For fuck's sake, do you want written permission?" I asked, knowing exactly how I sounded and caring approximately zero.

Before I realized what was happening, I found myself on my back on the sofa with Santi on top of me, taking my mouth again. It was probably a good idea. Who knew what else would come out of it. Better to keep it busy.

"I like this Micah. Assertive. Sure of what he wants," Santi said, trailing a path of kisses down my neck and over my shirt.

"Temporary insanity. Your fault."

He raised his upper body and removed his shirt—well, my shirt—those sexy hard abs that I'd avoided staring at earlier on the beach were now in front of me.

I needed to lick them, so I tried to sit up, but Santi pushed me back down.

"Nuh-uh, you stay there."

He lifted my shirt up to my arms and over my head. My instinct was to breathe in and tighten my stomach, which I knew wouldn't make a difference to how I looked.

Santi looked like he wanted to say something. I stopped breathing, waiting for the rejection, for him to realize this wasn't what he wanted after all.

He lowered his head onto my chest and inhaled deeply, then kissed every inch he could reach.

I could feel tears in the backs of my eyes trying to make their way out. My dick had deflated, and I was way too emotional, considering this was meant to be just two guys getting down and dirty.

Except Santi wasn't doing that. He was showing me exactly how much he wanted me while his dick remained hard against my leg.

When he came up to take my mouth again, I banished the ghosts once more.

I opened my legs so he could fit between them. As his cock rubbed against mine, even with two layers of shorts between us, my dick sprung back to life with a fierceness that scared me a little.

"Santi...I..."

"Fucking tight shorts. Micah, tell me I can take them off. My blood supply is severely compromised here."

I nodded but didn't wait for him to do it. It wasn't until I helped him push down his shorts that I realized how tight they were on him.

My apology never left me because the sight of his long, hard cock, the purple head ready to blow, and the thatch of dark hair at the base had me completely mute.

He kept still as I reached out to touch it and then hissed when I wrapped my hand around the hard shaft. Santi's cock was as smooth as velvet, but there was no mistaking the hard core of it would be strong enough to drive me insane.

I looked at him. His eyes were half-lidded, and he was

biting his lip as if trying to stay in control. I tightened my grip and dragged it up and down a few times, feeling on top of the world when Santi started moving against my hand.

One single move with my other hand got my cock out. It was impossible to hold us both with one hand, so I pulled his hip down to align our cocks.

"Is this what you want, Micah?"

"Yes...fuck, yes, Santi."

"God, I love when you say my name like that."

He placed a small kiss on my lips and kneeled up. I was about to complain at the lack of contact when he removed my shorts and his all the way before settling back between my legs.

He wrapped his arms around my shoulders and whispered in my ear, "This is going to be hard and fast, okay? I'm already on the edge."

I nodded and opened my legs more, wrapping them around his waist as much as my big thighs allowed.

"Fuck, I love that," he groaned.

Santi did all the moving since I was trapped under his weight. He took both my hands and placed them over my head, keeping them there with one of his hands.

The other gripped the underside of my leg.

He moved against me, our cocks lubricating each other with the precum we were both leaking.

"Santi," I gasped.

I was so close, and he was moaning against my neck like he was exactly where I was.

"Kiss me, Santiago."

He claimed my mouth in a bruising kiss and increased the pace. His hand gripped my leg harder as he pushed me further into the couch. I'd end up with my body permanently etched into it.

"Micah...fuck, I'm coming."

Santi stilled, and I felt the warmth of his release all over my cock and stomach.

My orgasm was right there beneath the surface. How I hadn't come already, I didn't know, but as soon as Santi moved his hand from my leg to grip my cock, that was all I needed.

I shouted my orgasm into his mouth, and he swallowed every single one of my cries.

Minutes later, my body was still humming, and Santi was still on top of me, having released my hands to hold me closer.

When we finally moved, there were no words exchanged. He kissed me and looked into my eyes as if he needed to make sure I was okay.

I'd never been more okay in my life.

We showered again in our separate bathrooms. I didn't know if Santi wanted to sleep with me or not, so I didn't ask.

When I went to the kitchen to grab a glass of water, I heard his soft snores from the guest bedroom.

I leaned against the wall outside and thought about what had just happened.

I'd just had sex. Me, Micah Sawyer, the almost thirty-year-old virgin, was no longer a virgin.

Okay, so it wasn't *sex* sex. Technically, if I considered only penetration as sex, then I'd lost my virginity at twenty when I'd finally gotten the guts to order a sex toy online. I'd blushed for a whole week after using it, certain that everyone could tell that I'd enjoyed penetration with a silicone dick.

To me, sex was the intimacy between two people. Being

naked together and bringing each other to climax. And we'd done that.

I liked to think that Santi's sleep had come so soon because he'd enjoyed it as much as I had.

It didn't matter that we hadn't cuddled after our showers or that instead of sleeping in my bed with me, he'd stayed in the guest bedroom.

There was no way I could deny our connection. Even the voices of my insecurities weren't strong enough to make me believe in them right now.

I walked back to my room and went to bed. Tomorrow was an important day, and I needed to rest. I checked the doggy cams on my phone one last time.

Olive was asleep, and somehow, Alfie had managed to sneak in and was cuddled up to her.

I put the phone down and turned the light off, hoping for dreams of Santi, his irresistible body, and addictive lips.

I turned the handle on the door slowly, thankful when it didn't make any noise. It was barely light outside, but enough that I didn't need to turn any lights on to go down the stairs.

The door to Micah's practice was open, as was the door to the recovery room where he'd placed Olive.

It didn't take me long to find out why when I saw Alfie peacefully asleep curled up next to Olive, who was awake and noticed me as soon as I walked in.

"Hey, Duchess," I said softly. "I hope your friend doesn't get in trouble with the sexy doctor."

She did one of her speech growls and licked my hand.

"It's a big day today. You be a good girl, and we'll be home soon, okay?"

She raised her head the way she always did when she didn't want me to stop scratching behind her ears. There was nothing I'd refuse her right now.

"I'm going to promise you this, Duchess. Live through this. Come home, and I'll let you have all the pets you want."

She let out a little bark.

"That's a dangerous promise to make. Most people would promise more treats or toys."

I turned around to see Micah leaning against the door-frame, wearing a ripped pair of jeans and a T-shirt with faded letters that I could just about make out saying, *Dogtor Sawyer*.

"She's a special girl," I said.

"That she is."

He came into the room and checked Olive while kicking Alfie out.

They both growled at him, which made me smile, but after licking Olive's face, Alfie left.

"Do you want coffee? Breakfast?" Micah asked.

He looked relaxed like this was just another day for him.

Part of me was annoyed because this wasn't just another day. My life could change again in just a few hours, so it wasn't just another day.

But at the same time, I was glad that he wasn't over-thinking what had happened last night. Or at least it didn't appear that he was.

I was doing enough of that for both of us.

Last night wasn't exactly a mistake. There was no denying we'd both wanted it to happen.

But Micah was inexperienced, and he deserved someone who could be there for him. I couldn't let him fall for me or expect more than I could give.

Micah deserved a man who'd take his arm for a walk by the river and talk about smart things. *Not* a veteran who'd take his arm because he couldn't see where he was going and didn't know how to have an intelligent conversation.

I knew how to flirt, to talk my way into and out of any situation, and to kill. I didn't even have a career anymore.

No, Micah would find his perfect partner.

All I could think was, *thank god I wouldn't see it happen*. Literally.

"Santi?"

"I'm sorry about yesterday," I blurted out.

Micah froze in place, but his face didn't change.

"What are you sorry for?"

"I took something from you."

Micah raised his hand. His brows were drawn together in anger.

"First of all, I'm not some old maiden who will be forever cast aside for being with a man before marriage. I'm not a woman, and this is not the early 1900s. Second of all, I've had dildos bigger than your dick inside my ass. Don't insult me by turning me into something I'm not."

He turned around and left the room.

I stood in place, confused until Olive nudged my hand.

"I'm a dick, aren't I?"

She growled her agreement.

"All right, you don't need to be so quick."

I went searching for Micah, but he wasn't anywhere in the clinic or his apartment.

I grabbed my shoes and went outside to the backyard. Maybe he was with his animals.

As soon as I stepped out of the back door to the porch, I was blinded by the sun.

"Fuck."

I closed my fists into balls. If I could punch anything, I would, but I knew it wouldn't change the outcome.

"Fuck it. I'll get used to being blind eventually." I took a few steps but miscalculated how far away the end of the porch was and ended up tripping on the step to the lawn.

I wanted to call out to Micah, but my pride made me

get up. Everything was blurry, but I could see where the dog fence was, so I walked to that and then felt my way to the small gate.

By the time I navigated the excited dogs and got to the other side, my eyesight had adjusted to the light.

The barn was empty, so I walked around to the back field.

Relief flooded my chest when I saw Micah standing in the field and staring out into the rising sun.

"I'm sorry, Micah. I'm so sorry."

He moved but didn't turn around, so I continued.

"I'm scared. I'm confused, and most of all, I'm a dick."

"You got that right."

I smiled. Shy Micah was adorable, but the assertive Micah really got my engine going.

"Tell me how much of a dick I am," I said, getting closer and wrapping my arms around him from behind.

He sighed. "It wasn't my choice to have never been with someone. Somehow, all the guys I met and had a connection with never wanted more. I have a string of failed dates that could wrap around the planet. I can't even count the times I was dumped before we got intimate, only to be told it was them, not me, and weeks later, I'd see them with a slimmer, prettier guy."

Micah paused, and I couldn't help tightening my arms around him. "Those guys missed out on a great relationship. Maybe I'm partial because you're exactly the kind of guy I like, but the guy who'd dump you for someone else has to be a special kind of asshole."

"That's just it, Santi. We had a great night. Yes, it was a first. No one has ever touched me like that. So don't ruin it for me. You said you took something from me..." He turned around. "You took the voices that tell me I'm not enough and made me feel like I'm a regular guy."

I put my hands on his face. "But you're not, Micah. You're far from regular. You're as special as they come. Tell me you hear my words."

He put his hands on mine and lowered them to rest between us. "I know what you're afraid of. That's why I wasn't upset when you didn't spend the night with me in my bed, even though that's what I wanted. I didn't bring last night up because I didn't want you to think I had any kind of expectations."

"And then I went and ruined it," I said.

He smiled. "Let's not overthink this. I don't expect anything else to happen between us. I don't expect you to profess your undying love for me. All I want is to feel like any other guy out there. If that means having a one-night stand, so be it."

I couldn't help pulling him into a tight hug.

"Thank you."

If only Micah knew how I wished things were different. If I wasn't losing my eyesight, I'd have claimed him as mine and never let him go.

"Come on, let's have a coffee and something to eat. April will be here soon, and she's going to ask why you're wearing beach shorts. You don't want to face that inquisition without caffeine."

I laughed and followed him back to the house.

Micah explained what he was going to do with Olive, so after breakfast, I went down to see her again before escaping to the barn.

An hour or so later, I'd moved the rest of the stuff from the barn and was looking at the empty space when Micah came in.

"Hey," I said.

"Hey. The vet tech from a practice in New Haven is on the way to assist me. I've checked both blood samples. She's as healthy as she can be to cope with his kind of operation, but there are still risks. I need you to understand that. She doesn't need the surgery, although it's likely she'll have a repeat of yesterday. That is a bigger risk because, without treatment, she could die within a few hours."

He'd already explained it to me, so I was pretty sure this was more for his benefit than mine. He wanted to be sure I understood the risks. That I trusted him but also knew there were many unknowns that could put Olive's life at risk.

I went over to him and took his hands, bringing them up to my lips.

"You can do this. I have no doubt, and I trust you."

"Okay. I'll come get you."

I nodded and couldn't resist placing a soft kiss on his lips.

He smiled and returned to the clinic.

I turned back to the barn and wondered what job would take my mind off of Olive's surgery.

My phone rang as I approached the barn, so I took it out of my pocket.

"Hello?"

"Good morning, is this Lieutenant Torres?"

I straightened my back at the woman's use of my title, not sure if out of habit or because lately it had come accompanied with bad news.

"Speaking."

"Lieutenant, I'm Doctor Amira Singh. I'm an ophthalmologist consultant for the VA. I was wondering if you had some time to see me at my practice."

"I appreciate the call, doctor, but unless you're going to tell me I'm not going blind, I won't bother."

"Lieutenant, have you ever heard of Choroideremia?" she asked.

"No."

"Choroideremia is often misdiagnosed as Retinitis Pigmentosa. There's a genetic test we can carry out to find out for sure."

I sat on the wood beams by the barn.

"What's the difference, doctor?" I asked.

"Treatment, Lieutenant."

MICAH

"Okay, let's close her up."

Calling my friend's practice to borrow her vet tech had been the right call. She was experienced, knew how to follow instructions, and was thorough.

I knew I needed to hire a tech, but I wasn't sure I could afford one just yet, especially now that I'd lost money to the construction company. Using the techs from neighboring practices worked for now and gave them some additional experience.

The last one that had helped me with an important surgery turned out to be eager to help, but a total chatterbox, which had been distracting. Something I couldn't have afforded today.

Mel grabbed what I'd needed and placed it all in order on the tray.

"I'll get these cleaned, doctor," she said, taking away the tray with the tools I'd been using.

"Thanks, Mel."

I didn't draw a proper breath until Olive was sutured and in recovery.

The surgery had gone as well as could be expected. There were a few times when Olive's blood pressure had dropped to a dangerously low level and given us a little scare, but she pulled through.

"That's it, all done. Is there anything else I can help you with? If you have other surgeries today, I'm happy to stay."

"Thanks, Mel. I don't have anything scheduled. You were great. I can see why Spence won't let you go," I said. I knew he wouldn't have declined my request, but he still took pleasure in making me beg for it.

Mel raised her hand, showing me her diamond ring now that she'd cleaned up and wasn't wearing the surgical gloves.

"He can't let me go now." She winked.

"The bastard," I said, standing up and giving her a hug. "Congratulations. I hope you know what you're getting into. I roomed with him in college, and I wouldn't wish his messy ass on anyone."

She laughed. "Don't worry, doctor. I'm only his assistant at work."

"Good. Tell him I expect an invite to the wedding. And any time you feel like a change of scenery, you have a place here."

She nodded and looked at the clock on the wall. "If you don't need anything, I'll get going. I want to stop by the square to grab some pastries from Spilled Beans before I head back to the city."

I chuckled. "You're a woman after my own heart, Mel. If my heart was that way inclined."

After Mel left, I updated my notes on Olive's file and went to check in on her.

Alfie was scratching at the window of the recovery

room, demanding to be let in, so I went outside and picked him up.

"You're lucky to see her before your daddy, but you can't stay, all right?"

He meowed, and I smiled to myself. I always talked to the animals, but they didn't always respond. It all depended on their personalities and life experiences. But it seemed Santi's pets were always happy to chat.

Olive was still on a table, so I placed Alfie by her head, staying with them as Alfie reassured himself that Olive was just sleeping.

"Come on, buddy. Time's up."

Alfie meowed.

"Fine, but you're out as soon as your daddy sees her. She needs to rest."

He purred, which I took as agreement to my terms.

I was cornered by April as I was leaving the recovery room.

"Doctor, Tom is here to see you."

"Olive has just come out of surgery, and I need to speak to Santi first."

She shrugged, looking apologetic.

I sighed.

"Do you want me to call Santi while you speak to Tom?" she asked.

"No, that's okay. Hopefully, this won't take long. I don't want to keep Santi waiting."

She smiled a knowing smile that I didn't like. My own feelings were confusing enough without adding her matchmaking.

"You stop that," I said, pointing at her. "Let's see what Crazy Sparkles wants."

Tom squealed as soon as he saw me.

"Micah, sweetie, you're going to loooove the news I have for you," he said, clapping his hands together.

"Matt Bomer is divorcing his husband and moving to Chester Falls," I deadpanned. "Troy will be pleased."

I tried not to snort, but Tom's confused expression was too amusing.

"Um...no, I don't think so. But if that's true, I'll throw him a divorce party that'll rival a Hollywood bash. You know how I love a challenge." He smiled. "Anyway...I've come from the Chamber of Commerce meeting. Ben proposed using the funds from this year's book fair to pay for the Rainbow Bachelor's Ball."

"I'm sorry, the what?"

He huffed. "The Rainbow Bachelor's Ball, to raise funds for your sanctuary, remember?"

"Yes, of course. I'm sorry, it's been a little crazy around here," I said. "Tom, I really appreciate you doing this. What can I do to help?"

"Not a thing, sweetie. All you have to do is turn up and bring your hot vet." He winked.

"My what?" I coughed.

"Oh, come on. Troy spilled the beans on you and Santi. Said you think he's hot, and then I saw you getting cozy at the market." He crossed his arms, daring me to deny.

"It's...it's not like that, Tom." I felt a blush crawl up my skin.

Fucking pasty complexion.

"Uh-huh, of course it's not. Just like rainbows aren't pretty and sparkles don't sparkle."

April stared at me trying to hide her smile and failing, so I pulled Tom into the examination room.

"Ooh are you going to tell me all the secrets," he sang. "I

promise I won't tell. Well, I'll tell Wren, but I'll tell him in bed, which means he's sworn to—"

"Tom," I interrupted. "Can I ask you something?"

"Anything, sweetie."

"Um...thing is..."

"Micah?"

I stopped at the sound of the voice behind me.

"Santi."

"Hey, big boy," Tom drawled, looking Santi up and down. "If you need a suit for the ball, just drop by Fabulize. I'll give you my friends discount. You'll need to look your best if you're dating the star of the show. Anyway, I have to get back to the store, so I'll leave you pretty boys to pick a color swatch for your coordinating suits. *Mwah*." He blew us a kiss and left in the same whirlwind he'd arrived in.

I let out a breath. "I'm sorry about that. I was going to call you, but then he turned up."

Santi sat on my desk chair. "How's Olive? Did she make it?"

I smiled and went over to him, kneeling by his legs and looking up at his worried expression.

"She's fine, Santi."

His shoulders sagged immediately as he let out a long breath.

I took his hands in mine. "Post-op is always challenging. Sometimes worse than the op itself, but I'm confident she'll make a full recovery. Do you want to see her?"

"Can I?" His eyes lit up like Christmas morning.

"Of course. She should be waking up soon. Believe it or not, you're not her first visitor," I chuckled.

Santi followed me into the recovery room. I knew he wouldn't relax completely until he saw her.

We both stopped as we surveyed the scene in front of us.

Olive was awake and letting out small growls at the attention she was being given by Alfie, who was licking her head as if she was his kitten.

She was likely very confused and wondering why she couldn't move much and felt a little queasy.

"Alfie, anything you want to confess?" I asked the kitten, but this time, he ignored me.

Gus and the new puppy, Doug, had somehow managed to get in the room and up on the table and were sitting by Olive's tail. At least in her groggy state, she wasn't wagging very hard.

Santi kneeled by the table and cradled Olive's head.

"I guess this is part of the agreement, isn't it, baby girl?" he said. "Although I was hoping you'd resume hoarding pets *after* you were back at home."

She growled again as if defying him.

I leaned against the wall and put my hands in my jeans pockets, feeling the hole at the bottom. The sight in front of me was the reason I'd become a vet. All the hours studying after volunteering in farms and vet practices, the sleepless nights, and the lack of social life. It had all been worth it to be able to sit back at this moment and watch as Santi spoke gently with Olive, making all kinds of promises and giving the other pets a little bit of attention as well.

They were a real family. It warmed my heart to know Santi had these animals' backs as much as they had his.

He turned around. "What happens now?"

"She'll need to stay here a few days so I can make sure she's recovering well from the surgery. There's some care needed after she goes home, but we can play it by ear. She can stay here as long as necessary."

Santi got up and came over to me, wrapping me in a tight hug. He smelled of freshly cut wood, and I wondered if he'd been doing something with the wooden beams my granddad had left in the barn.

I held on to his T-shirt, leaving him to decide when to step away from me.

He didn't. I was starting to wonder if he was really okay when I thought I felt something warm and wet against my neck.

"Santi," I whispered.

He didn't reply, but he kissed the same area and then kept kissing until he reached my mouth. He sucked my lips into his mouth until I had no choice but to open up and allow his tongue inside to massage mine. My body lit up like the fourth of July.

"Micah," he whispered against my lips. "Thank you."

I opened my eyes to find his boring into mine.

"Hey, it's going to be okay," I reassured.

He nodded and stepped back. Enough to no longer be pressing me against the wall but still very much in my space. As was his erection.

I sighed. "Santi..."

"Can I stay the night again? I promise to behave. I just... I can't stand the thought of being home alone when she's here."

"Okay."

After the call from Doctor Singh and then seeing Olive awake from her surgery, I needed the walk home to process my thoughts.

Olive was okay. She'd survived the surgery and was loving the attention from all her friends. Micah said dogs were usually a little moody after surgery because they were confused about what had happened to them.

Not my beautiful girl. I needed to research how close to humans dogs were because I was pretty sure Olive was more human than dog. Hell, even Alfie and Gus, not to mention Doug.

I sighed, knowing there was no way Gus would come home without Doug, and since the last thing Micah needed was another animal to look after, I was starting to accept I'd be adopting the little Boston Terrier.

"Dude, wait up."

I looked across the road and saw Wren Mason wave.

"Sup, man?" I asked as he fell into step with me.

"Eh, the usual. Tom says you've been spending a lot of time with the hot vet."

I looked at him and raised a brow. He laughed and held up his hands.

"Sorry, are we not allowed to acknowledge how pretty Micah is? My bad."

I took a side step to tackle him. He was quick, but I had all the combat training, so even with my rapidly increasing tunnel vision, I still had him in a headlock before he could call uncle.

"Don't you have a bunch of kids to boss around? Or your fiancé, for that matter?" I asked, releasing him.

He laughed. "No one bosses Tom. Not unless you want to keep your dick attached and glitter-free."

"I really don't need to know what you do in the bedroom," I deadpanned.

He wiggled his brows.

I shook my head.

"Anyway, the guys are meeting up for drinks at The Falls on Friday. Why don't you and the hot, sorry, sexy, sorry...um...vet join us?"

He ran off laughing before I could tackle him.

"Eight-thirty," he shouted from across the road.

Would Micah want to go to The Falls?

He worked too hard, first setting up his practice and then looking after all the animals that were left in his care.

I wasn't sure he had much of a social life. When we'd met that day by the river, he'd been on his own, and I hadn't seen him mention any friends other than his vet friend from New Haven.

Maybe it would be good for both of us to go.

I was going to see Doctor Singh in a couple of days. If the test results came in fast, maybe...

Maybe Friday could be the start of something with Micah.

I grabbed a few changes of clothes and put them in my duffle bag before making my way back to Micah's place, taking a detour via Spilled Beans, where I picked up enough pastries for a battalion.

April almost offered to have my babies when she saw me enter the clinic with the pastry box.

"He's with a patient at the moment, but I'll make sure he has a break after," she said.

"I'll drop this upstairs and head out back. See you later, April."

"Uh-huh. Staying over again, I see."

I leaned over her reception desk, flexing my arms as I rested my hands over the edge.

"Jealous?"

She leaned back in her chair and crossed her arms.

"Son, you wouldn't know where to begin with a woman like me. Stick to the kind doctor." Then she leaned forward. "But you hurt him, and you'll have to deal with me."

I laughed and gave her a kiss on the cheek before leaving her, but her words of warning stayed with me longer than I cared to admit.

Hurting Micah was not something I'd ever knowingly do...but was I already doing it?

~

"Lieutenant, lieutenant!"

"What?" I opened my eyes slowly. My head was pounding.

"Lieutenant, we're under attack."

I sat up, taking in my surroundings. What the fuck was I doing in a tent?

The noise of fire finally came through to my senses, and what was that smell?

I started getting dressed. Why the fuck wasn't I dressed? I always slept with one eye open and ready to fight.

"Santi. Stay down."

More machine gun noises.

"Ryan? What are you doing here?"

"Huh? You on drugs or what? We gotta save Luca. Hurry up!"

The mention of my brother's name was like a shot up my ass to get ready. For some reason, my moves were uncoordinated and much slower than usual. It was as if I hadn't trained in months.

"Where is he?" I demanded.

"In the tent with all the explosives we seized. If they get to him and the explosives, he's dead, Santi. Fuck, I never got to tell him I love him."

That made me pause. "What are you talking about? You two are engaged. You've been together since Christmas."

"That shit's not funny, Santi. Come on, on three..."

I followed Ryan out of the tent. We shot our way out toward Luca. There were tents on fire, men dead on the ground.

"Ryan. Down."

The man in the corner of my eye moved, giving away his position. With a single shot, I took him out.

"Santi, Ryan, over here."

Luca was sheltering behind an ammo truck.

"What happened?" I asked when we got to him.

"Fuck knows. Someone must have given us up. I was doing the rounds, it was quiet, and next thing, I'm being shot at."

Ryan started patting Luca.

"Stop, man, you're giving me a hard-on."

"Shut up and tell me you're okay, Luca. I can't live without you," Ryan growled.

My instinct told me something was wrong. Very wrong.

"We gotta go. Everyone's dead." I turned to the deep voice and found myself staring at James.

A piercing pain shot through my head. I closed my eyes and squeezed my head with my hands.

"Fuck, have I been shot?"

"Santi..."

I opened my eyes at the sound of the soft voice in my ear.

"I can't see anything. Luca. Ryan. What's happening? Why can't I see?"

"Santi, please..."

I tried to feel for what was around me, but there was nothing. No truck. No Luca. No Ryan. No James.

"Why is this happening?" I cried.

"Santi, wake up."

"I'm not fucking asleep. Do I look asleep? Why am I blind?"

"Santi, please."

The voice sounded so worried. And what was that smell? Pine? Lemon? It smelled good.

"Santi, you're worrying me. Please wake up."

My chest felt like it was on fire. I opened my eyes.

"Micah?"

"Thank fuck," he said, cradling my face and turning me to face him. "Are you okay?"

"I...don't know." I coughed.

I moved in the bed and felt my shirt completely drenched against my body. The bedsheets were all twisted around my legs.

Micah lay down next to me and pulled me into his chest.

"Wanna talk about it?"

"It was...I don't know...a mix of nightmare and reality, I guess. I woke up in an army tent, but nothing was as it should be."

"Like what?"

"I couldn't react or move. Everything was slow. Then Ryan came in saying Luca needed help. We were under attack."

The anxiety of the dream came back, so I closed my eyes and held on to Micah.

"It was only a dream, Santi. They're all safe, and so are you." He ran his hand over my hair.

"I was blind, Micah. I couldn't go anywhere or do anything. I was useless to help them."

"Santi, can I do something for you?" he asked.

I looked up at him. "You already do so much, Micah."

"Not like this, come on." He sat up, taking me with him. Then he took my hand and pulled me toward his room.

It was much bigger than the guest bedroom. There was a king-size bed, a dresser, a closet, and a chair by the window. Nothing else.

"I haven't gotten around to decorating. I want to paint the walls but haven't picked a color yet," he said, almost embarrassed.

"I can do it for you."

He smiled. "I didn't say it so you would do it."

He took two towels from the closet and pulled me to the bathroom, which was a carbon copy of the one in the guest bedroom but with a bigger shower.

"Get naked," he ordered.

"What?"

"You heard me." Micah took off his shirt and boxer briefs.

I did as he said. I wasn't going to argue against being naked with him, but I didn't understand it.

He turned the water on, and when it was to temperature, he pushed me in and followed behind.

"What time is it?" I asked.

"Just past three in the morning."

"Fuck, I'm so sorry I woke you up."

He smiled and grabbed the shower soap, lathering it in his hand before running it over my shoulders.

"Hmm, that feels good," I moaned, letting my head fall to the side, enjoying the warm spray of the shower.

"Good. Now listen to me. Being blind isn't a death sentence, Santi. Many people live happy and satisfying lives without their eyesight."

I sighed. "I don't know if I know how to accept it, Micah. I'm used to being in charge, helping people, fighting for my country. I don't even know who I am anymore."

He turned me to face him, and I tried to forget that we were both naked in the shower with a layer of slippery soap between us.

"Santi, you are the man who stopped to check if I was okay. You are a man who accepts new pets into your family just because it makes your dog happy. You are also a man who fought bravely for our country, but that doesn't define you. I wish you could accept that you can still have everything you want whether or not you can see it with your own eyes."

"What if what I want is you, Micah?"

I focused on his eyes, framed by wet lashes and freckles. His hair dripping and darker than usual.

He took my hands and placed them on his face.

"Close your eyes," he said, and I obeyed.

"Can you still see me?"

I swallowed the emotion that was stuck in my throat. Using my fingers, I traced the lines of his cheeks, his nose, his lips. I felt as he closed his eyes when I ran my fingers over his lids. I pushed his hair back and memorized the curve of his neck as I pulled him closer.

"I can see you," I whispered.

"Then you can have me, Santi."

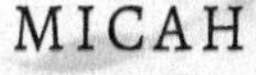

MICAH

Santi's dark eyes were as vulnerable as I'd ever seen them. I wanted to take his pain away, but I knew it wasn't down to me. He needed to believe it himself.

"I got a call from an ophthalmologist today. A consultant from the VA," he said.

"Oh yeah?"

He grabbed the showerhead to rinse the soap from us and then turned the water off. I got out of the shower and picked up the towels I'd taken from my closet earlier.

"She thinks there's a possibility that I could have been misdiagnosed."

"Can that happen?"

"Apparently so. I have Retinitis Pigmentosa. That's when the photoreceptors don't work the way they're supposed to, and over time, you lose your sight. It's passed on from parent to child, which is where my case gets complicated because no one in my family has it."

"So what else could it be?"

Santi wrapped his towel around his waist. I did the same and guided him to my bedroom.

"Get in," I said.

His slow smile gave me butterflies. He flipped his towel off, showing me his erection, and jumped on the bed.

I laughed. "If you think you're getting lucky, you've got another think coming."

"Are you sleeping in this bed with me?" he asked.

"Yes."

"Then I'm already lucky."

I shook my head and got under the covers. He pulled me into his arms, which felt a lot nicer than it had any right to be. This man was going to be the death of me.

"Okay, so tell me about this other diagnosis," I said.

"I don't know much yet, and I definitely can't remember the name the doctor said on the phone. I can do some genetic tests or something. If it turns out I have the other condition, there's a treatment."

I trailed a path over his chest with my finger, unsure of what to say. This was good news. If he could keep his sight or at least not have it get worse, that would be great.

But I didn't want him to think that was the only acceptable outcome.

"How do you feel about it?" I asked.

"Don't know...I'm as scared of hoping for treatment as I am of losing my sight forever."

"How much research have you done about your original diagnosis?"

In the dark of the bedroom, I could feel Santi looking down at me, even if he couldn't see me.

"Not much. I was...trying to avoid it. Why?"

"Dogs can also have RP. The difference is that there is treatment. When you mentioned your sight problems, I did some research. Yes, if you have RP, you're likely to go blind, but it can also take a long time for that to happen. I read a blog post from this journalist that was diagnosed twenty years ago. While she's legally blind, she does have some sight. The way she explains it is as if she's looking through the gap of a letter box."

I let my words sink in.

Santi was silent for a long time.

"Could you finish work early on Friday?" he asked.

"I can check. If not, I'm sure I can move some appointments. Why?"

"I'd like to take you on a date and then out with the guys. When was the last time you were at The Falls?"

My smile was so wide that it was a good thing Santi couldn't see it.

He wanted to take me out on a date.

I tried not to read too much into it, which was not easy, considering we were also naked in my bed.

"I'd like that very much."

"Good." He yawned, which made me yawn.

I don't know which one of us fell asleep first, but I know we didn't move an inch for the rest of the night because I woke up with my head on Santi's chest and his arms still around me.

Somehow in my sleep, I'd thrown a leg over his and had decided that humping him was a good idea. I mean, there were worse ideas to have.

"You better stop that before I have to do something about it." His sleepy voice was even deeper than usual, but it carried a softness I hadn't heard before.

My stomach tightened in anticipation. "What...what if I don't stop?"

He growled and turned us so he was on top of me.

"Morning," he said before slamming his lips on mine for

a kiss that got me hot from the top of my head to the tips of my toes.

His erection rubbed against mine.

"Argh, Santi," I moaned.

"Shh, baby, let me take care of you."

"It won't take long if you keep doing that," I said.

He kissed a trail down my chest, rubbing his hands over my belly.

"Fuck, I love how soft you are. How much of you there is. You're fucking perfect, Micah."

I bit my lip, unable to speak as he inched closer to my dick.

"God, even your cock is perfect," he rasped. "One day, I'm going to have you filling me with this thick dick, but I need to taste you today."

I had to grab onto the sheet because I was about to come in the most embarrassing way.

Santi held on to the base of my cock, which helped to keep the orgasm at bay. He even knew how to do that.

"Look at me, Micah. I want you to watch."

"I can't...I'll come too quick."

He chuckled, and I felt the air from his mouth ghost the head of my cock. "That's the whole point, baby. Come in my mouth or on my face. I don't care. I just want you to enjoy."

"San—argh!" My call became a cry when he lowered his mouth onto my cock until I felt it hit the back of his throat.

He pulled off slowly, dragging his teeth over the skin of my sensitive shaft before sucking on the crown.

When his eyes raised to meet mine, I couldn't hold it any longer. I came hard and fast into his mouth. My hips raised, fucking into his mouth.

He swallowed every single drop and then came up for a kiss.

"Touch me, Micah, please..."

Even in my blissful, post-orgasmic state, I found enough energy to move, but Santi put his hand on my chest to keep me down.

"With your hand. I need to kiss you."

I reached down to where he was humping against my thigh and gripped his erection. I may not have been experienced with other men, but I knew what I liked.

He thrust into my hand at the same time that I twisted my wrist and ran my thumb over his frenulum.

"Fuck...Micah!" he shouted, and then I felt his warm release all over my hand and thigh.

"Well, that was quicker than I thought," I joked.

He slapped my arm but then pulled me closer and kissed me some more.

"Inexperienced my ass. You're fucking lethal, baby," he said.

I didn't miss how he'd called me baby a few times now. Even though I didn't want to make a big deal out of it in my head, I couldn't help feeling giddy whenever I heard the word.

How many times had I dreamed of this precise moment? Being someone's baby, honey, sweetheart, anything.

Chill out, Micah. Don't go all Stepford wife on the guy.

"Come on, we need to get up and grab a shower," I said, slapping his tight ass.

He chuckled. "You're a dangerous man, Micah Sawyer."

"Who? Me?" I asked, sauntering to the bathroom stark-naked.

Who was this Micah? I didn't know, but I liked him. And I liked how Santi made me feel.

Whether this was the start of something or a one-off, I was determined to enjoy it.

After visiting Olive, Santi stayed in the barn all day. I took him a sandwich and a drink for his lunch, but he wouldn't let me get close to the barn. Instead, we sat on the porch.

Even April decided to enjoy the sunshine and ate her lunch with Salt, Pepper, and Alfie for company while I tended the reception area.

Olive was doing well. There was no sign of infection, and she was eating all her meals. Once a day, we allowed her friends to visit, which was quite ridiculous, but I couldn't deny that she was always in a much better mood afterward.

Somehow Santi ended up staying over the rest of the week. We stopped the pretense that he was staying in the guest bedroom after the second night.

It made sense for him to stay since he was still working hard in the barn. The animals were happy here, and he could see Olive any time.

The night after his appointment with Doctor Singh, Santi had been quieter than usual. I didn't push him to talk because I knew he was likely trying to process the potential outcome of the genetic exam.

We'd gone to bed early, and he'd rested his head on my chest, running his hands over my belly until he fell asleep. In the middle of the night, I woke up to find him gone, but a quick check of the doggy cams showed him talking to Olive.

I'd put my phone down and gone back to sleep. In the morning, he was cuddled up against my back.

As for sex...well, it had been plenty...of the same we'd

already done. I was ready for more but didn't know how to ask for it.

My insecurities sometimes got the best of me, but I tried to squash them. Santi was going through a hard time, and to want more sex was, quite frankly, selfish.

So I happily waited for our date, wondering if this meant we were casually dating or if we were boyfriends.

"Doctor Sawyer?" April asked from the door.

"Yes?"

"There's a woman here asking to speak to you."

"Okay, is it a patient? I thought I didn't have any more appointments today." In fact, I was about to turn off my computer to go get ready for my date with Santi.

"No, she says she knows you. Christy Reynolds?"

I froze in my chair.

"What?"

"Shall I send her away?" April had a worried look on her face.

"No, that's okay, send her in."

I took a deep breath and readied myself to face the grown up version of the girl who kickstarted the bullying campaign against me.

SANTI

I stretched out my back, hearing the satisfying crack. Who knew building tiny houses was so much hard work.

Micah's grandad was a true hoarder, but I'd have to admit that it was fun figuring out ways to use some of the stuff he had.

I couldn't wait to show Micah what I'd been working on.

After he'd shown me the designs he had for the sanctuary, I knew there was a lot I wouldn't be able to do. In order to house different animals, he'd need metal fencing and gates, but the inside of each area could be customized to make it a good home for the animals.

The dog houses were first since there was more than enough wood. Micah had approved my rough sketches, but what he didn't know was that I'd also bought paint from Mason's general store so each of the houses was individual.

I'd found some rope that I wrapped around a few wooden stakes, added different platforms to it, and they made awesome cat play areas.

The more time I spent with Micah, the more I knew he deserved this and more. He was beyond generous with his time, and he cared so much for his patients and their owners. No wonder his waiting room was always full.

Granted, most were women who just adored him. They talked about his grandad and how Micah was following in his steps. I was starting to think it was some kind of Sawyer cult.

One last check that everything was in place, and it was time to get ready.

I walked over to the clinic, hoping to drag Micah into the shower with me, but stopped when I heard voices.

His consultation room door was open, which was unusual when he had someone with him.

"We were kids, Christy. I don't know what you want from me," Micah said.

Christy?

I searched my brain to remember where I'd heard that name before.

"Do you know how embarrassing it was? I was one of the most popular girls, and afterward, no guy wanted to date me because they didn't want to turn out gay."

Ah...that Christy...

I didn't need to hear Micah's sigh to know how he was reacting to her ignorant words. Like the classy guy he was.

Her voice grated on me. I couldn't even imagine how Micah felt from close up.

"I want you to publicly apologize to me," she said.

"I beg your pardon?"

"I. Want. You. To. Apologize." She marked each of her words.

What was it about her and her posse that made me want to hit women? Ah yeah, their shining personalities.

"Are you on drugs or something? You and your friends started a bullying campaign against me, all because I didn't want to make out with you because I. Am. Gay."

Pride filled my chest when I heard Micah.

Christy whined.

"You didn't have to do anything. Do you think I would have told anyone? You started it, and thanks to you, the rest of high school was a living nightmare. So no, I'm not apologizing to you now or ever. Please, leave my premises."

I heard his chair roll off. He must have stood.

"Listen here, you fat faggot. You put an apology in the local paper, or else. You have no idea who you're dealing with. My husband is about to be voted mayor of Chester Falls. What do you think will happen to your little rat's nest here? Huh?"

Her voice was more poisonous than a viper, and I couldn't hold it any longer.

I marched in, ignoring Micah, and walked straight up to her.

"Santi. So it's true," she said, crossing her arms and staring at me with a satisfied grin.

"What is?" I asked.

"You two." She pointed to both of us and then made a disgusted face.

"For someone that doesn't like gay men, you seem quite fixated on us. And so is your cousin. Does it have to do, by any chance, with your husbands enjoying each other's company? You know, playing the hide-the-sausage game?" I turned to Micah. "Who do you think plays hide and who plays seek, baby?"

Christy gave us a stare that would have evaporated us if she could and then turned around to leave. When she was by the door, she turned her head back. "Good luck with your little fundraiser."

I followed behind her to make sure she left the building and then told April to close up and go home.

When I went back into the examination room, Micah was in the same place, shaking like a leaf with his eyes fixed on the ground.

"Hey," I said gently, running my hands up and down his arms.

"She's going to have me closed down, all because I wouldn't kiss her when I was a kid. This isn't happening, is it?"

"Look at me, baby," I said, shaking him a little so he'd look into my eyes. "Her closet-case husband will never be voted in, and even if he is, have you seen the line of people that come by to see you every day? The town will have your back."

"Do you really think so?"

"Yes."

"Is her husband really in the closet?" he asked.

I laughed. "Let's put it this way: my last summer before I enlisted was a lot of fun."

Micah looked down again, but this time I knew it was for a different reason.

"Baby, what I meant was that I caught him and her cousin's husband-to-be engaging in a game of tonsil tennis with a happy ending. My guess is they never came out and went on to marry the girls."

"That's...quite sad. I mean, for all of them. I can't imagine having to pretend to be someone else," Micah said.

"And that's what makes you special, baby." I pulled him a little closer.

"I like it when you call me that. No one's ever given me a nickname."

I groaned. "You're gonna kill me, Micah Sawyer. Stop being so damned adorable."

He grinned, so I kissed the grin right off his face.

"Come on, let's go upstairs. We need a shower," I said.

"We?" he chuckled.

"Uh-huh."

We stopped by the recovery room to check on Olive. She was drinking from her water bowl. Alfie was curled up to Doug and Gus on her bed.

Micah went to the closet in the hallway and grabbed a dog bed for Olive so she wouldn't end up on the floor.

When she saw her new quarters, she sniffed all around it and lay down. Then she growled, and her friends got up from their bed to join her.

"This can't be normal. Tell me this isn't normal."

Micah laughed. "She's a social animal, so it's natural for her to draw in other pets. Ducks are also very social and like to live in groups. I guess they all decided they were going to be their own little family."

I wrapped my arms around him. "They know a good thing when they see it."

He leaned into my chest, so I kissed his hair.

"Do we really have to go to The Falls?" he asked.

"Not if you don't want to. We can do whatever you want."

"Um..." he let out a sigh. "Never mind, we should go. Tom's working so hard on the fundraiser, it would be rude to not join them."

"Okay."

If I thought I was going to get lucky in the shower, I

was sorely mistaken. Even though Micah had let me wash him, and we kissed a lot, he hadn't even gotten hard.

There was something on his mind that I couldn't decipher, and that was bothering me.

He stood in front of his closet for the longest time, staring at his clothes before picking a pair of jeans and a T-shirt I'd seen him wear a number of times.

"Micah, is everything—?" My phone interrupted me. I looked at the screen to find Luca's name across it.

"Hey, Luca, can I call you back? I'm in the middle of something."

"Can you and *Something* buy me dinner? Your fridge is in a sad, sad state."

I froze. "What?"

"You heard me. Benny's Diner. Thirty minutes. I'm sure you can find a satisfactory pause for you and *Something* in time to meet me there."

He hung up, leaving me to stare at the screen.

"Ugh, Micah, I'm really sorry, but I have to go. Can we meet at The Falls later?"

"Okay."

I leaned over to meet his eyes. "Are you really coming? I'll make it worth your while."

He smiled and nodded.

"Good." I got dressed quickly and called a cab. Benny's was on the other side of town, so I'd never make it in time if I walked. Especially not at sundown.

When the cab honked to let me know of its presence, I kissed Micah hard and made him promise to meet me later.

In ten minutes, I was at Benny's, reading through the menu while waiting for my brother.

"I'm loving the reception party you put out for me."

I turned away from the menu at the sound of Luca's voice.

He stood there with a big smile, and I forgot I was mildly annoyed with him for turning up unannounced.

"Come here, you little fucker." I stood and wrapped my arms around him. "Missed you, dude."

"Oh really? I wouldn't have thought so, considering how often you answer your phone. I had more success when you were out in the desert."

He sat across from me in the booth and picked up a menu.

"I'm starving. Kris's airplane is comfortable, but a guy my size can't live on the rabbit food they serve there. Besides, Momma Ruth's pancakes are a mandatory first stop in Chester Falls."

I laughed. "Look at you moaning about flying in a private jet. Eighteen months ago, you ate dust and loved it."

His smile left his face. "I never loved it, Santi. I just couldn't stand to be away from you and Ryan."

"How is he?"

The smile returned tenfold and something squeezed in my heart.

"He's good."

"So, you gonna tell me what you're doing here, or do I have to guess?"

"I'm working on the security team for your boyfriend's fundraiser, so I came early to see James. The plane has gone back and will return with Kris, Charlie, and Ryan next week."

I had so many questions. I didn't even know where to start.

My boyfriend?

How did he know about Micah? Also, was Micah my

boyfriend? Hell, I'd spent so much time fighting our attraction before giving in that I hadn't thought about what exactly it was we were doing.

And why would it take him a whole week to plan security for the event? Having the Prince of Lydovia and his husband attending was a big deal, but James had worked for Kris, and I knew how good he was. Between Luca and James, it wouldn't take them more than a couple of days to put everything together.

Which could only mean one thing.

Luca was back because of me.

Shit.

MICAH

Ugh, you're such a fucking loser, Micah.

No wonder Santi had taken off at the first chance he got.

Christy's visit and threats had done a number on me. At that moment, I'd been the vulnerable teenager who didn't understand why people were saying all those horrible things about me. Why there were messages on my locker, and why no one ever approached me to ask what had really happened.

But then Santi came along and saved the day like a real knight in shorts and a tight T-shirt. I really trusted his belief that Christy and her husband couldn't do anything to harm my business.

If her husband really was gay or bi, but in the closet, then there was no way he'd risk bringing attention to himself. And that was even if he was voted in. From what I gathered, the current mayor was a popular guy and was considering running for reelection.

So with that problem gone, I had a new one. I was a

little anxious about my date with Santi and especially our subsequent meetup with the guys.

We'd all gone to the same school, but the ones in my year, like Wren and Connor, had spent more time on the football field. While they'd been friendly toward me, we hadn't necessarily been friends.

We were all acquaintances more than anything else, and I was terrified I'd be awkward and not know what to talk about. They all knew each other well, and I would stand out.

In my rising anxiety, I wondered if I could just spend time with Santi, but just like I was scared of asking him to take the next step in bed, I didn't want to admit to being a total awkward-sauce when it came to socializing.

I'd tried being more social in college. That had been my fresh start where no one knew me. But it had failed miserably, so I gave up on college parties and focused on my studies instead.

With Santi gone, it was clear our date was canceled, or at least on a raincheck. I changed the sheets on the beds in both rooms and tidied up.

When my stomach rumbled, I couldn't face any food, so I grabbed my favorite ice cream from the freezer. Even that wasn't enough to calm my nerves.

It was a sad state of affairs when ice cream didn't help me anymore.

Deciding what time to arrive at The Falls was another stressor. Did I arrive early so I could establish a one-on-one conversation with the first ones arriving? But then I'd be the sad, lonely figure until they got there.

Maybe I'll just stay home.

"No, you promised Santi. Pull your pants up and go."

The pep talk was kidding no one, but I still got in the

car and drove to The Falls, which was just on the edge of town.

There were plenty of cars in the parking lot, which wasn't surprising on a Friday night. I'd only ever been to The Falls when Spence stayed over during college break and dragged me to the bar.

It hadn't changed much since the last time I was here. Same dark wood and leather-covered seats. Same pool table in the corner, and I'd guess the people here were also the same.

Even though I was unsure of myself in these situations, I appreciated the bar for what it was. A good gathering place for the locals.

I noticed a hand waving and turned to see Tom calling me. He was at a table with Wren, Indy, and a big guy I'd never met before, but if I took a guess, that would be Indy's husband, Tate.

"Hey," I said, approaching the table. Santi hadn't arrived yet, so I was unsure of what to do. "Shall I get a round? What are you drinking?"

That was a good question, right? Everyone loved a free drink.

"We have it on good account that drinks are on Santi tonight," Wren said, pointing to a chair for me to sit.

I took a step but stopped when I felt a large figure behind me. In that soft tone I'd only ever heard aimed at me, Santi said, "Hey, baby. So glad you came."

A shiver went up my spine, making me weak at the knees. He turned me around and claimed my mouth in a kiss that was basically a neon sign informing the world that I belonged to Santi Torres.

"Jesus, Santi," I whispered when he finally released me.

He kissed my nose and turned to the guys, keeping his arms around me as he spoke.

"That's in case you fuckers want to start placing any bets. Yes, I know your dirty little gambling act."

"Too late, dude," Wren said and then turned to the table. "Pay up, suckers."

Tom looked visibly deflated, but Wren whispered something in his ear that made his cheeks blush and his smile return.

"This isn't fair," Indy moaned. "I own the best coffee shop in town. It's a rule that I should know all the gossip first." He crossed his arms.

"Don't worry, baby, you're still my love doctor," the big guy said.

He turned to me and extended his hand. "I don't think we've met before. I'm Tate."

"He's Micah, and you can put your big hand on your husband," Santi said, taking the hand I was holding out to meet Tate's. I stared at him with my mouth open and an explosion of butterflies going on in my belly.

Santi took a seat, pulling me so tight, I was dangerously close to sitting on his lap.

"What do you drink?" Santi asked.

"Oh, um, I'm driving, so soda is fine."

He pulled out his phone and sent a message, placing it back on the table before looking up toward the bar.

I looked the same way and saw Luca waving and giving a thumbs-up.

"Luca's here?"

"Yeah, he's the reason I had to bail on our date. Don't worry. He's paying for at least two rounds of drinks to make up for it."

Everyone cheered when Luca came over with the

drinks, and there were multiple questions about his new job as a special guard for the Prince of Lydovia.

I struggled to keep track of everything once Santi had explained that Charlie Williams, who'd been in the same class as me, was now a prince by marriage. Charlie had been in the army with not only Luca and Ryan, but also James, who went to college with Kris, *the prince*, and subsequently became his head of security before falling in love with Connor, Charlie's brother, and moving back home.

"My head is spinning, and I'm not even drinking alcohol," I said. "I wasn't aware there were so many LGBT guys in our school, and now everyone's paired up."

"Ugh, tell me about it. I'm struggling to find enough bachelors for the auction," Tom said, putting his cocktail down. "What am I going to do?"

"I can't help because I'm very happily married," Indy said.

"Damn right," Tate added.

"But I can volunteer my brother. Sage would love to help you," Indy said.

Everyone laughed.

"No, he wouldn't," Tom said.

"Write his name down." Indy pointed at Tom's little notebook he'd taken out. "Sage Birch. Oh, and..." he looked at Tate. Tate opened his eyes wide and a smile spread over his mouth.

"Harrison Davis," they said at the same time.

Whoever this Harrison guy was, I was already feeling sorry for him for being dropped into the bachelor auction.

Hold on, would they want me to do it too?

"Okay, that's two more. Keep thinking, people."

"Um...Tom...do I have to..." I trailed, not wanting to

voice it but also feeling guilty that my name hadn't come up.

"No," Santi said. "You're not being auctioned."

"He's not," Tom said. "But you are." He pointed his glittery pen at Santi.

They kept throwing names at Tom, even mentioning Troy at some point, saying it was for a good cause, and he loved animals, so he'd be up for it.

Wren reminded everyone that Troy was still a minor. No matter how grown-up he acted most of the time.

As the evening progressed, I felt more and more relaxed. I wasn't sure if it was because the group was friendly and I was able to join in their conversation, or if it was because, with Santi's arm resting on the back of my chair and his hand caressing my arm, I felt safe, happy, like one of the guys.

Santi's phone lit up, and I couldn't help notice the email notification. His hand froze on my arm at the same time that he looked at the screen.

"Gotta go to the big-boys room. Can I get anyone a round on my way back?" he asked.

There was a round of yesses. Santi stood and left the table.

Everyone was chatting, so they didn't notice he'd gone toward the balcony and not the restroom. I excused myself and followed him.

I found him leaning over the wooden rail of the balcony area, staring at the river below.

"Hey, everything okay?" I asked.

He turned around, gripping the phone in his hand.

"Doctor Singh emailed the results... I can't look at it, Micah."

I took a step closer. "Do you want me to open it for you?"

He handed me the unlocked phone. "Please."

I took a deep breath and opened the email.

My heart broke for Santi when, even before I opened the attachment, I read in Doctor Singh's note that his RP diagnosis had been correct.

She was positive that, like in most cases, Santi was likely to retain some vision for most of his life, and there was some medication, as well as vitamins, that could help slow down the progress of the degeneration of his retina. She would like to see him to discuss those options in more detail.

I couldn't help the tear that ran down my cheek. "I'm so sorry."

I put my arms around Santi, but he pushed me away.

"Don't feel sorry for me," he bit back.

"I don—"

"Nothing's changed. I guess this is as good a time as any to enjoy the rest of my life."

He turned around and went straight for the bar, bumping into a couple of people on the way but not seeming to care.

I followed him, but he ignored my presence. He ordered a few shots and downed them one after the other, then he ordered two rounds of drinks.

The bartender looked at me, but all I could do was nod. I had a feeling this wasn't going to be pretty, but there was no way I'd let Santi go through this alone, whether he knew it or not.

He returned to the table with the tray of drinks, setting it down before announcing.

"So, I'm going fucking blind. Let's celebrate."

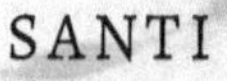

SANTI

My head was pounding, or maybe someone was pounding at it and making it hurt. Either way, I felt like shit.

The arm around my waist tightened and the warm body moved closer.

Micah. Fuck, why do I feel so rough?

I moved his arm carefully and managed to keep my eyes open long enough to walk to the bathroom without bumping into anything.

Once I relieved myself, I brushed my teeth and washed my face. The cold water was a relief, but I needed some dry toast and painkillers, or I'd be suffering the rest of the day.

"Hey." Micah stood by the door. "How are you feeling?"

"Like someone who drank far too much last night, made a fool of himself, and hurt his brother in the process."

He came close and wrapped his arms around my waist, leaning into my chest.

"He's okay. I had a message from Wren. Luca stayed with him and Tom last night because he was too drunk to be home on his own since I brought you here. Between the two of you, you had enough alcohol to burn an entire village. I'm surprised you're upright."

"Just about," I confessed. "He's really mad at me, isn't he?"

Micah raised his head to meet my eyes. "He'll live. He's hurting because he just got the news, but you're the one dealing with it, so you're entitled to feel the way you do. Come on, let's get something into you."

I raised my brows, and he laughed. "I meant food."

"Shame," I said, bending down to kiss him.

After breakfast, I called Wren, but he said Luca didn't want to talk to me. I told him I'd stop by there in the afternoon whether Luca wanted to see me or not. Even if he refused to talk, I still owed Wren and Tom an apology for turning last night's outing into Santi's Big Pity Party.

"Want to see Olive? She's been calling for you," Micah said.

The way he was trying to keep me busy was so endearing.

Olive was once again surrounded by all her friends. She'd recovered from the surgery, but we couldn't allow her outside by herself in case she got excited playing with her friends and hurt herself.

"Hey, baby girl and troublemakers." They all looked up at us and came over for their share of human petting.

It still amazed me how these animals had built a connection with each other. It didn't matter that they were different species. They found their own way to communicate.

Micah and I sat on the floor of the recovery room as Alfie, Gus, Doug, and even Olive played with us. Micah's face was so full of joy.

Despite everything, and especially after last night, Micah was still here. He'd looked after me.

I'd seen the pain in his eyes when he read the email. He didn't cry because the result wasn't what he'd expected. It didn't matter to him that I was going blind. He'd cried because he knew how this would make me feel.

It was time for me to be a better man. It was time to give myself to him in the way we both deserved.

I took his hand from where it was petting Doug and held it up. Micah took my lead and got up with me. We went up the stairs to his apartment, stopping in the kitchen to wash our hands from playing with the pets.

"What's going on?" he asked.

"Come sit with me...actually no, come sit on me." I went over to the couch and pulled him by his hips so he'd straddle me.

He placed his hands on my chest but then wrapped them around my neck when I buried my head in his neck, kissing and sucking his creamy skin.

I loved how pliant he was under my touch. Micah was guarded, and I had a feeling he didn't show himself to just anyone. It was a testament to the trust and rightness of our relationship that I was allowed to see the real Micah.

His lips were as soft as always, with that little bit of scratch from his beard heightening all my senses.

"Micah, I need you," I moaned into his mouth.

He leaned further into me. Our erections rubbed against each other, even with the layers of clothing between them.

"I need you too," he said.

"No, Micah. I *need* you."

He broke our kiss to look at me. "Does that mean... what exactly does that mean?"

"It means I want you to fuck me. I want to feel you inside me."

"But...I thought..."

His adorable face was a picture of all the emotions running through him. He wanted this, but he was scared.

"I'm versatile, and even though it's been a while, I have bottomed before. But I want to have a first with you that I've never had with anyone else."

"I don't understand."

"Would you blindfold me? I don't know what the future holds for me. Despite my reaction yesterday, I do understand the options, and I know I may have some kind of vision for a long while. But with the loss of my vision, however little it may be, I will fumble, I will trip. If I'm going to do those things, if I'm going to learn how to live with this, then I can't think of anyone else I'd want to do it with than you." He stared at me. "Micah, I need to know it's not only okay to not be perfect, but it can also be good too. Let's fumble together, yeah?"

I raised my hips, and he gasped. "Fumble together?"

"Uh-huh."

"Bedroom. Now," he rasped.

"At your service." I put my hands on his round, delectable ass and stood, taking him with me.

He shrieked. "Put me down. I'm too heavy."

"Baby, I've carried gear heavier than you in over one-hundred-degree heat. You're a sexy feather to me."

Micah removed his shirt even before we made it to the bedroom, then wrapped it around my head to cover my eyes.

"Do you want to reach the destination first?" I asked.

"Nope, the journey is the best thing. You remember the way."

I did remember the way to his bedroom, but with him sucking on my neck and the scent of his shower soap all over my face, you couldn't blame a guy for struggling to keep it together.

Fortunately, there weren't many bumps. At least until we reached the bed. I bumped against the frame with my shins, which caused me to lose balance, and we both fell on the mattress.

He turned us around so he was the one on top, and then he helped me undress.

My shirt became another layer over my eyes that made everything even darker.

"You're so gorgeous, Santi. All of these hard muscles show your strength, but only I know how soft you can be." He kissed a trail over my sternum before sucking on one nipple and then the other.

My dick was begging for some kind of relief, but Micah was in charge. He would decide when it was time to get fully naked.

Having my eyes covered heightened everything else around me. I tried to decipher where Micah was going next by listening to the way he moved. Every time he licked or sucked a patch of skin, my belly tightened as I wished for him to keep moving south.

When my shorts and underwear were finally removed, I almost shouted in relief, canting my hips in search of some friction. My cock felt like it was harder than it had ever been.

I missed Micah's presence near me and then heard what sounded like a drawer opening and closing.

The bed dipped again, and shortly after, my cock was engulfed in tight, wet heat.

"Fuuuck, Micah."

In the few times we'd been together, Micah hadn't gone down on me. It was just one of the stupid barriers I'd put up to make it easier to move away from him. As if I ever could.

"You can't tell me you've never done that before," I said.

"What can I say? I'm a fast learner, and your cock is perfect."

He nudged my legs, which I took as a sign to open up for him. I raised my legs, hooking my hands under my knees to lift them up.

I was more exposed than I'd ever been with anyone because not only was I on full display for Micah, I couldn't see him. I didn't even know if he was still dressed. The thought scared me, but it also freed me to just let go.

"One of these days, I'm going to eat you like my favorite ice cream, Santi. But not today because I'm too wound up by the thought of being in you, and you look like you're about to combust."

"You're not wrong," I said.

I heard the noise of a cap opening and soon after felt the coolness of the lube on my hole. Micah's fingers followed.

First teasing around the rim and then slowly easing their way in.

"I need you to tell me if it doesn't feel right, okay? I'm only doing what feels right to me because I don't know another way," he said.

"Fuck, you're doing just fine. Give me more."

I felt the burn more than if I'd had my full eyesight because every tiny move of Micah's fingers in and out of me was blown out of proportion.

"You're so tight, Santi."

"Don't worry, baby. It's gonna fit so good. Let me touch you."

His body draped over mine until I felt his warm breath on my lips. Hot, wetness traced my lips. I opened my mouth, hoping to have a taste of him, but instead, I let out a strangled moan when he pressed his fingers against my prostate.

"Micah." I swear I saw stars in the back of my eyes. This was going to be over too damn soon.

I kissed him and touched him wherever I could in the position I was in. His cock was hard and unmistakably wet with precum.

"I'm ready," he whispered into my lips.

The sound of foil tearing was like a promise. Whatever happened, we were each other's firsts.

Micah's hand shook against my thigh. I took a deep breath and relaxed as much as I could to make this easier on both of us.

The pressure of his cockhead against my hole made my stomach tighten, but I pushed against it until he made it through the ring of muscles.

He'd stretched me enough that once I caught my breath, I needed more of him.

"Fuck, Santi." His tight voice sounded just like I felt. On the edge.

"Give me more, Micah. All the way."

He inched slowly, and in the dark, it felt like his dick was never-ending. Beneath the T-shirts, my eyes were closed and my brows drawn to cope with the intensity of being with Micah like this.

As soon as I felt his balls against my taint, I pulled him to me and wrapped my legs around him.

"Fuck me, Micah."

I had one arm around his shoulders and the other on the back of his neck. We kissed as Micah drove in and out of my body, making me feel every single fiber of my being.

I could only imagine what we looked like together. Funnily enough, I didn't need to see it because I knew in my mind and my heart that we looked perfect.

Mostly because it wasn't about how we looked but how we felt.

As my orgasm built to the point of no return, all I could think was that I was going to make sure Micah knew every day how much I wanted him, how perfect and beautiful he was to me.

We were barely scratching the surface of our lives together.

This was just the beginning.

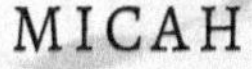

MICAH

Being inside Santi felt too good to be true. I was either dreaming or in some kind of alternative-reality game. Since I'd never been into gaming, I'd have to conclude I was dreaming.

I fucking hoped I came before I woke up, or I'd be really pissed.

Santi tightened the grip of his thighs around me, so the only part of me that could move was where we were connected by my cock in his ass, and even then, I could only manage small thrusts.

His ass was so hot and tight. If my nuts didn't burst, my head would for sure.

"Micah...Micah..." Santi had a strong grip on my hair, to the point of pain. It was likely the only thing stopping me from coming. If I stopped thinking about how good he felt, this would be over.

"Is it always this good?" I rasped in his ear.

"No," he said between strained breaths. "Definitely not."

His words surged through me, giving me power I never

thought I'd have. Any doubts that I wouldn't be good at sex or that I wouldn't know what to do were pushed aside.

Maybe it was because this was what we were all born to do. It was instinct. Or maybe it was because this was Santi and me, and anything between us would always be better than good.

I pulled back as far as I could without pulling out completely and then thrust in with one stroke.

"Micah!"

I gritted my teeth and did it again, spurred on by Santi's whimpers as I hit his prostate with each thrust.

Santi shook beneath me, and then I felt his release between us. He hadn't even touched himself.

Two more thrusts and I finally let go, coming in Santi's tight channel in an orgasm that seemed to never end.

Even before I could regain my breath, I needed more of Santi, so I pulled the shirts from his head and kissed him. He squeezed his eyes shut, adjusting to the bright light of the midday sun streaming in through the window.

When he finally opened his eyes, and those dark brown orbs stared at me, I knew... I'd fallen in love with Santiago Torres.

"Jesus, baby. If this is our first, I'm not sure how we'll live through the rest," he said, yawning into my neck.

I pulled out carefully, but he still winced. After removing and disposing of the condom, I got a wet cloth to clean Santi. By the time I reached him, he was asleep, so I cleaned him and then snuggled up to him.

He'd slept fitfully the night before because of the alcohol, so neither of us had had a great night.

I must not have realized I'd also fallen asleep because the next time I opened my eyes, I was staring into Santi's sexy face.

"Hey," he said, cupping my cheek with his hand.

"Hey, yourself."

"God, I love waking up to you."

"You do?" I asked. He hadn't complained before, but it was still nice to know he liked sharing my bed.

"Very much so. How about we grab a carton of that delicious ice cream you have in your freezer?" he asked.

If I hadn't already known I was in love with Santi, *that* would have done it.

I leaned on my elbow and put my leg over his. "Wait...is this a trick so you end up eating the ice cream off me?"

He smiled. "It wasn't, but now I know you have the best ideas."

I kissed him and then moved down to his chest, licking his nipples as I made my way over to lick his tight abs. The man was hard muscle everywhere.

"See? What did I say? *The* best ideas."

I chuckled and stopped.

"Tease," he said, pouting, which looked way too adorable for a man of Santi's size.

"On a serious note. We should talk about yesterday, and you should talk to your brother."

He sighed. "What do you want to know?"

"Are you really okay with the results of the genetic testing?"

"As okay as anyone can be with the knowledge that their life is going to change forever. All the things I've been doing for you in the barn will become an impossibility. I guess that's what scares me the most. Up until now, I was ignoring it, pretending it wasn't happening. But I can't do that anymore, and I don't want to. But what will I do with the rest of my life?"

I cradled his cheek and ran my thumb over his two-day-old scruff.

"You don't have to have everything figured out at once. I think it's more important for your own mental health to accept that change is coming. That'll make you stronger to face the change."

He raised his hand, tracing my temple and moving down my cheek to stroke my beard.

"You make me stronger, Micah."

"Me? I'm a socially-challenged veterinarian nerd," I laughed. "How can I make anyone stronger?"

He gave me a smile that was as warm and soft as if he'd wrapped me in cotton wool.

"I don't care how long it takes me, Micah, but I'm going to make you see what I see. The caring vet who's lost all his money but still wants to save all the animals he can, the friend who sees past the disability and believes I can be more. God, Micah...you're..." He sighed as if he didn't have words to express what he wanted to say.

"How about Luca?" I asked, changing the subject because the more he talked, the closer I got to blurting out my love for him, and I was terrified it was far too early.

"Let me show you something I've been working on. Then we'll go to Wren and Tom's place."

"Ice cream first?"

"Absolutely. But not from your body, or we'd be in bed all of next week."

It was the weekend, and as such, it was totally acceptable to have ice cream for lunch, or at least that's what I told myself.

After we more or less inhaled a whole carton of chocolate-and-peanut butter ice cream, we checked in on all the animals and put Olive on a leash. We were going to let her have some light exercise today.

"Am I finally going to see the big secret you've been working on?" I asked as I followed Santi through the backyard.

"Yes, but we need your target audience for final approval."

He opened the gate of the dog enclosure that lead to the back and the barn beyond the hedge. My heart skipped a beat, but it seemed the dogs were all following Santi.

As he pulled the large barn door open, the dogs ran inside. Olive stayed by my side.

"Oh my...Santi. I have no words. You did all this...? It's beautiful."

I stared at the beginning of my dream coming true before my eyes. Colorful dog houses were decorated with some of the stuff my grandad had kept all those years and happy dogs. Everyone deserved a home, and whether it was modest or wealthy, the important thing was that it was happy.

Santi broke the distance between us and wrapped his arms around me. Tears flooded my eyes. How could I ever thank Santi for everything he'd done to help me realize my dream? For helping me get that tiny bit closer.

"It'll be perfect when it's all finished. Your designs and ideas are great. As soon as you have the support from the fundraiser, we can get the structural materials you need to create the separate areas."

"I don't even know what to say."

"Say you'll fumble with me later. I'll even buy you dinner before."

I hit his chest, but there wasn't much strength behind

it. I was always a sure thing when it came to fumbling with Santi.

The dogs obeyed when it was time to return to their secure area. When had that happened? Had Santi been training them, or were they just so used to having him around that it was second nature?

And then I thought, *I could get used to having him around too.*

We dropped by Wren and Tom's place mid-afternoon. Wren led us to their living room, where Luca sat on the couch with Coco on his lap, looking like the queen she was.

His eyes were sad when he saw Santi, but then he put Coco down and walked over to his big brother, holding him so tight it made Santi catch his breath.

"I'm going to sit with Tom and Wren and give you some time," I said.

He nodded, not letting go of his brother, but leaned over and gave me a soft kiss on the lips.

Tom was taking a tray out of the oven as Wren and I walked into the kitchen.

"Coffee?" Wren asked.

"Please. Thanks," I said.

Tom put the tray down on a cooling rack and turned to me.

"Sooooo, you're playing doctor with the hot veteran..."

I snorted. "I'm a vet. That just sounds wrong."

Wren placed three cups of coffee on the table and sat next to Tom. "How's he doing?"

"He'll tell you himself, but he seems okay. It's not easy coming to terms with something as life-altering as this."

"I know," Wren said. "I thought I had my whole life planned out. I was on top of the world, and then everything came crashing down when I had my injury. It's definitely not comparable to vision loss, especially since the only thing the injury did was end my pro career, but it certainly felt that way in the beginning."

"What changed for you?" I asked.

"I walked past a group of kids playing on the street. I hated them because they didn't know how lucky they were. Something kept me coming back, and eventually, one of them recognized me and asked me for some tips. That was the first step into accepting that even though I'd left football, football hadn't left me. I went back to school to do my degree in education, and next thing I knew, I was a high school coach."

"Are you happy?" That was the crux of it. What if Santi didn't find his true happiness? What if I wasn't enough for him after a while?

I hated myself for having such a selfish thought.

"I don't know what my life would be like if I hadn't been injured, and I don't even entertain the thought. My life has turned out so much better than I ever imagined." He looked at Tom with so much love. "And I have a purpose. Maybe one of the kids I train will become the next Peyton Manning. Maybe they'll find the same joy that I do in football, even if they end up as lawyers, accountants, chefs, whatever."

I nodded.

"Alright my little sparkly unicorns, I am caffeinated, and the happy brownies are almost cool enough to eat," Tom said.

"Happy brownies? Please tell me that doesn't mean what I think it does," I laughed.

"Sugar is my only drug, sweetie. That and Wren, of course. Now go stand over there while I feel you up."

I coughed, and Wren snorted. "He means he's going to take your measurements."

"What for?"

"The gorgeous suit I'm making you for the fundraiser, of course," Tom said, rolling his eyes. He took a tape measure from a drawer and a little notebook from his pocket. The same notebook he'd had at the bar last night.

I didn't dare tell him there was no need for it, but I could see Tom wasn't going to budge.

For the next few minutes, I was handled like a puppet as Tom measured me head to toe before he kneeled and ran the tape measure up the inside of my leg.

"Hey, get your hands off my boyfriend."

I stared at Santi with my mouth open. Did he just call me…?

"Shut up, big guy. You're next," Tom said without moving an inch away from me.

Santi's dark eyes were so full of heat I was pretty sure I'd combust if I didn't look away.

Please don't get hard. Please don't get hard.

"Oh my god, are those brownies?" Luca said. He looked a lot more relaxed, and the happy smile I'd always known him to have was back.

"No, my dear. They're happy brownies," Tom clarified.

Luca's eyes went wide, and I laughed.

As soon as Tom stood, Santi walked up to me and wrapped his arms around my waist.

"I don't need happy brownies. I have all the happiness right here."

Luca pretended to gag, Tom gasped, and I laughed some more.

SANTI

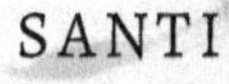

The designated parking area at Lexington-Bennett Hall was so full, Micah had to go around a few times to find a free spot for his car.

In the last week, as the countdown to the fundraiser started, there had been a lot of activity around the clinic. Micah had been interviewed by the local radio station, he'd been in the paper, and people had come over offering to foster the animals.

My work moved from the barn to the clinic, where I helped April manage anyone wanting to foster or adopt the pets. That allowed April and Micah to focus on their real patients.

Mindy's kittens all had new forever homes as soon as they were old enough to leave their mommy. Micah had decided that Mindy, Salt, and Pepper could stay with him since they'd been at the clinic from the day he'd opened.

Stella was adopted by a nice family who understood her health requirements and fell in love with the good-natured dog.

It was all going well until we had a few additions. A

cranky old dog that had lived with his owner until she'd passed away. Since there was no one to look after the dog, he was taken to the clinic, and he was not impressed with his new quarters.

We had a parrot, which caused a little last-minute panic because Micah didn't have a spare cage, and the pet couldn't be with the parrots he already had because he wouldn't stop cursing.

It was a busy week, but I didn't remember laughing so much in my entire life. Being around Micah was now so natural. It was as if we'd known each other for years and been together just as long.

With Luca around, I wanted to make the best of the time I could spend with him, so I'd been sleeping at home. Every morning, I'd walk to the clinic with Olive, Alfie, Doug, and Gus, and in the evening, we'd walk all the way back.

I'd tried leaving them at the clinic or at home, but wherever Olive went, they all followed. It was ridiculous and fucking weird, but this was the new Santi.

"What are you thinking about?" Micah asked. I hadn't even noticed he was taking his seatbelt off, ready to go inside.

I looked at him in his bespoke Tom Jones suit. He looked stunning, but I couldn't wait to get him out of it. Stolen kisses between appointments and one hand job when I dragged him up to his apartment at lunchtime a couple of days ago wasn't enough to get my fill of him.

"I was thinking about how I want to peel that suit off you later and wondering how early is too early to leave."

He took my hand and placed it on his lap. I squeezed his erection and leaned over to kiss him, delighting in the fact I could take things much further later.

Thank god Ryan was back today.

He'd flown in, and it seemed Kris, Charlie, Ryan, and one other guard were going straight to the fundraiser. The prince and his husband would fly back straight away, and Ryan would stay with Luca another week before they went back to Lydovia.

"Come on. Let's go in," he said.

I'd only ever seen photos of this place, but they never did justice to what the building was really like, and it was clear Tom had gone all out for this event.

The event room was decorated as if this was a fancy ball, but the tables were what showcased what the event was all about.

Each table had a photo of one of Micah's shelter animals, and behind each photo was their story. I didn't know when the photos had been taken, but it must have been when I was out working in the barn or when I had my appointment with Doctor Singh.

There were other little touches, such as bowls with dog-bone-shaped candy and pens that had cat ears on them.

Micah picked up one of the paddles from the table. "What kind of event is this?"

The sip of champagne I'd just had almost come out of my nose when I snorted. I leaned over and whispered in his ear. "If you take one of those home, I'll use it on you later." Then I sucked a bit of skin from his neck, feeling as he shivered and then melted into my touch.

"You're terrible," he said.

"You don't even know how much," I winked.

"Promise?"

I took his hand and brought it up to my mouth to place a kiss on each knuckle. "I promise."

Since our first proper night together, Micah's confidence had grown. There were still moments when I'd caught him worrying about his weight, like when he would put a shirt on and then decide it was a little tight. Or when he refused a small scoop of ice cream after dinner, saying he'd eaten too much, even when I knew he'd skipped lunch.

I wanted him to be happy, and if losing a few pounds made him happy, then I'd support him, but I could tell that it didn't. Missing out on a small portion of his favorite thing made him miserable, and life was too short for that.

We were both a work in progress, but in the same way Micah hadn't given up on me even knowing I was officially a disabled person, I would never give up trying to help him accept himself.

"Baby, James is over there. I'm going to have a quick word, okay?" I said to Micah.

"Sure. Wren just messaged to say he's on his way, and Tom is joining us as soon as he introduces the evening's events."

On my way to James, I saw Indy and Tate arrive, so I pointed them toward our table, feeling better that Micah wouldn't be on his own for too long.

James nodded as he saw me approach. "Hey, all good at your table?"

"Yeah, all good. Can't say I'm excited with the prospect of being auctioned off to some old lady with roaming hands, but I'll do anything to support Micah."

He smiled. "It's good, isn't it?"

"What is?"

"Finding that person that you can be yourself with, calls you on your shit, is always up for naked Sundays, and most of all, lets you love them unconditionally and returns the feeling."

I laughed. James had described exactly how I felt about

Micah, and I hoped Micah felt the same way. We hadn't actually said the words, but I had no doubt that the feeling was there.

It didn't matter that we'd only known each other for a month, at most. When you know, you know.

"Man, you're truly whipped," he said when I failed to respond.

"On a serious note, have you seen or heard anything about Christy and Jenny?"

"No. Luca spent some time around town during the week, scoping out the gossip. Turns out Christy's husband really is running for mayor, so I don't think she'd put his running into jeopardy with a scandal. If she's crazy enough to do it, we'll stop her before she gets her feet on the property, and you've seen how long that driveway is. They'll never make it up here."

"Good. That's a relief. I don't want those vipers anywhere near Micah. The stuff they've said about him..." Just the thought made my blood boil, so it was better to talk about something else. "Have Kris, Charlie, and Ryan arrived yet?"

"Yeah, just got the heads-up on the radio. Zeke's here too. I miss the crazy dude. Do you think we can convince them to stay an extra night? We could have a boys' night out."

I laughed. "If anyone can make that happen, it's your husband. Get Connor onto Charlie and release Tom on Kris."

James snorted. "Wren would kill me."

I returned to the table in time to see Tom kick-off the evening.

A local band played music while dinner was served. The food was amazing, and Tom told us he'd gotten Mary,

James's house manager who'd practically raised him, to manage the catering team and use her recipes.

My nerves shot up when Tom stood to get back on stage to start the auction.

"Dear friends and family of Chester Falls, it is time. Our bachelors are dressed up, groomed, and sparkly ready to be at your service. You know the rules. Be respectful, and unless you have consent, only touch parts that won't get you in trouble." He put his hand over his eyes to look for someone in the audience. "That includes you, Mrs. Rosenberg. Don't pretend you can't hear me. The rules still stand."

Everyone laughed. Tom was funny at the best of times, so he was perfect as the MC. Besides, with the guests being mostly residents of Chester Falls and clearly loving Tom, I was confident the fundraiser would be a success for Micah.

"The first bachelor on stage is a friend of a friend. He's here on totally false pretenses, so let's welcome him with a roar of applause. Welcome to the stage, Harrison Davis. Harrison is a lawyer who specializes in family law. He's a single dad of the smartest little girl. Harrison is happy to receive bids from the ladies or the gentlemen of the audience, so let's begin."

I watched with curiosity as various people bid on Tate and Indy's friend. One guy, in particular, seemed determined to win. The guy definitely knew how to wear a suit, but his long, straight blond hair that fell slightly on his face made me wonder if he spent more time in casual clothing.

"Is it me, or does Harrison look a little confused about the attention he's getting from that guy?" Micah asked.

"Good," Tate said. "He needs someone to rattle his cage, and I think Long Hair might just be the man to do it."

"Going once," Tom said into the microphone. "Going twice. Sold to the delightful gentleman at table twelve."

The guy stood to meet Harrison, who looked like he'd rather be elsewhere. I didn't miss the look he gave Tate when he glanced our way as he left the stage.

"Our bachelor and his date have the chance to spend some one-on-one time tonight in the greenhouse lounge before agreeing to a proper date. If you fancy yourself the chance, then open up those purse strings. Remember, it's all for a good cause."

Tom auctioned off a few more bachelors before there was a short break.

I turned to Micah. "I have to go backstage."

He looked a little deflated. "Okay...um...good luck."

"Hey, look at me. What's up?"

He scratched his beard as he looked into my eyes and smiled. "Nothing, just a little nervous for you. Good luck out there."

"I hope I don't get the old deaf lady with the roaming hands," I said.

His smile went a little wider. "I hope you do."

"You'll pay for that later," I said, giving him a quick kiss before joining Tom and the other bachelors backstage.

MICAH

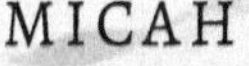

I knew it was stupid to be jealous, but the thought of seeing Santi with someone else made me feel physically sick.

"Hey," Indy said, reaching over the table and putting his hand on mine. "You know this is just for fun, right? He's going home with you."

"Am I that transparent?"

"Nah, we've all been there."

"You had to watch Tate being auctioned?" I asked.

He laughed. "Worse. We got drunk-married in Vegas after agreeing to keep it casual. You can imagine how that went down."

I shook my head.

"Like a bag of stale cinnamon buns. Not mine though. Mine are so delicious, I don't think I've ever seen a single one go stale."

I laughed. "That I believe."

"Chill and enjoy the show. You'll have something to tease him for later. I bet Mrs. Rosenberg will get him. She's lost every single one so far, and she's a feisty old lady."

"I think I'll go to the restroom to freshen up before they start again," I said.

Indy was right. I had nothing to worry about.

Micah: I have it on good authority that Mrs. Rosenberg is determined to get you.

Santi: Fuck. You better make it up to me later.

Micah: You can count on it. You'll be lucky to get past the kitchen before I'm inside you. I've missed your ass so much.

Santi: Thanks for the visual. If Mrs. Rosenberg thinks my hard-on is for her, I'm going to kill you!

Even though the restroom was empty, I went into a cubicle. My normal fashion was jeans and old T-shirts, so wearing a suit, a bespoke one at that, required more care.

I hung the jacket on the hook behind the door and unzipped my trousers. The suit was surprisingly comfortable, and I had to admit it looked good on me. Tom was such a talented designer and tailor.

Once I did my business, I took the time to unbutton the waistcoat so I could tuck my shirt in properly.

Someone came into the restroom. This guy, whoever he was, sounded like he was on the phone.

I ignored it until I recognized a name.

"Yeah, you won't believe it. Santi is getting auctioned at this event...uh-huh. I'm going to give him so much shit for it...yeah...last Christmas. You could say that we have unfinished business...yeah...I never thought playing tourist guide would be so much fun."

My stomach tightened, and I froze in place. The guy knew Santi.

Not only that, it sounded like they were close. Like, biblical close.

"He's a fun guy...no, I don't know if he's back here for good, but I'm sure I could convince him to move to Lydovia. After all, his brother and best friend live there, so it would make sense...oh, now there's a thought. Ryan and Luca are catching up now. If Santi is up when I get back out there, I'm going to bid on him. After such a long flight, I could do with chilling out a little before I'm back on duty... yeah...sure...kay, speak tomorrow."

I heard the tap going, and a moment later, the door to the restroom opened and closed again.

My hands shook as I buttoned up the waistcoat and put my jacket on.

I washed my hands and splashed some water on my face, then took a deep breath and went back out.

Indy and Tate weren't at the table when I got back, and Wren was talking to his parents, who sat with Troy at a different table.

Great. Thanks for leaving me to freak out on my own.

The lights dimmed a little, and Tom returned to the stage.

"I hope you're all freshened up and ready for more. We've already raised a considerable amount for our upcoming Chester Falls animal sanctuary, but those of you who have pets, you know the ongoing costs of caring for them. Now imagine you have twenty of them and some with special healthcare needs."

There were a lot of nods from the audience, and I wondered how many of these people had known my grandad and had come as a show of support for a project that was long overdue.

"Without further ado, let's begin the second part of our bachelor auction. Some of you might agree that we've left the best for last. Now, personally, I think all our bachelors are equally fabulous." He put his hand to the side of his mouth and pretended to whisper to the microphone. "I hear things in the greenhouse lounge are heating up. We could have romance on the horizon for some of our bachelors. Be still my sparkly rainbow little heart. Don't miss out on the ones that are left."

More laughs from the audience and people picked up their paddles and raised them to show how ready they were.

Tom called the next bachelor on stage, and I was relieved it wasn't Santi. I filled my glass with water and took a sip as someone came to stand behind my chair. I turned to see who it was.

"Oh my gosh, Charlie. It's been such a long time," I said in a low voice, not wanting to draw attention from the activities on stage.

Charlie gave me a quick hug before sitting next to me. "I know, right. This is Kris, my husband," he said, looking at the guy who took the next seat.

I waved, unsure of how to greet a prince, especially one that was the definition of tall, dark, and handsome.

Don't make a fool of yourself, Micah.

"You don't need to be nervous," Charlie whispered in my ear. "He's got all the same bad habits as any other guy you'll meet. He just makes up for it by being stupid gorgeous."

Kris winked, proving he'd not only heard Charlie but that Charlie was right.

I covered my mouth with my hand to keep myself from

laughing. Even though I hadn't met Kris before, I'd heard rumors about how down-to-earth he was whenever he visited Chester Falls with Charlie. Everyone in town seemed to adore the prince that stole the heart of one of our own.

I turned back to the stage to see the bachelor being led to the sunroom by his date, who had a happy smug face on.

My nerves rose again. I needed Santi's auction to be over as much as I was dreading it.

Tom delightedly announced the updated amount that had been raised so far on a screen next to him. People were allowed to make extra donations by writing them on a card they passed to the waiters that went around making sure everyone's glasses were full.

Every time Tom updated the number on the screen, it went up by way more than what had been raised through the auction. At this rate, I'd have enough to build the divisions inside the barn and look at building an enclosure for larger animals.

I'd had a horse rescue months ago that I'd fortunately been able to find a forever home for, but it wouldn't always be possible or a quick process.

I was also toying with the idea of having some kind of petting farm and offer school visits to educate children on the responsibilities of owning a pet. A large number of the pets that had been brought to me were perfectly healthy pets that had just become too much for people who'd given in to a child's request to have a pet, and it had turned out to be the wrong decision.

My thoughts about the future plans for the sanctuary were a welcome respite from my other thoughts about the bachelor auction, but as soon as Santi was called on stage, all my nerves returned.

"Oh, that's a nice suit," Charlie said. "I bet it's one of Tom's."

Santi's eyes roamed the audience. He looked visibly nervous, but when he saw me, he smiled. I smiled back and mouthed *good luck*. He then must have seen Charlie and Kris with me because he gave an almost imperceptible nod as Charlie waved at him.

"My fabulous friends, this fine specimen of a man is an army veteran with muscles that go on for days. I should know. I made his suit." Tom winked at the audience, and everyone laughed. "Raise your paddles if you want the chance to spend some time with Santiago Torres."

Every time a paddle went up, my heart rate increased.

Someone shouted, "Three thousand dollars," and I recognized the voice immediately as the guy I'd overheard in the restroom.

It was easy to spot the man because, unlike all the other guests tonight, he wasn't sitting at a table. He leaned against the back wall of the room, without a paddle in his hand, standing with the kind of confidence you didn't gain from validation. No, this guy was born with it.

He was blond and had blue eyes that were light enough that the color was visible under the light of the many chandeliers. He looked to be about my height, but that was the only similarity between us because his perfectly fitting suit didn't have a small bulge where his belly was like mine did.

His was flat, which highlighted the bulk of his chest and arms. Simply put, the guy looked like he could be a model.

All the things Santi had told me about liking my body were forgotten when I saw Santi's face as he looked at the guy and smiled. A genuine Santi smile.

A lady, who I assumed was Mrs. Rosenberg, looked at the guy like she wanted to murder him. She raised her paddle to increase the bid, but the guy outbid her straight away.

"Three thousand five hundred."

"Three thousand seven hundred."

I watched Santi as he kept his eyes on the guy. Did he want the guy to win?

Mrs. Rosenberg was getting progressively annoyed if the redness on her face was anything to go by. "Ten thousand dollars."

"Eleven thousand dollars."

The bidding war between Mrs. Rosenberg and the guy went on until they reached thirty thousand. There was a part of me who was delighted for the sanctuary, but right now, the part of me who didn't want the guy to go anywhere near Santi was winning.

The room felt too hot and full of people. I drank more water and wondered when this would be over, but it all seemed like it was going in slow motion. I didn't remember the bidding for the other bachelors taking this long.

They reached thirty-five thousand and stopped when Mrs. Rosenberg tapped out.

"And we have a very generous winner. Come on over to get your bachelor, sir."

The guy walked to the stage as if he owned the room.

Santi more or less ran down the stairs where the two met in an embrace. The guy gave Santi a kiss on the cheek and whispered something in his ear. Santi drew his head back in laughter.

"Baby, let's match Zeke's bid," Charlie said to Kris.

What? They know the guy?

"Done. I just hope I don't have to fire him again because those two together are trouble. The maids still haven't recovered from seeing him cross the lawn as naked as the day he was born," Kris said.

"They lie. I've caught them talking about it, and how big Zeke's...you-know-what is."

They both laughed, but I couldn't join them or even muster more than enough words to excuse myself.

The guy—Zeke, apparently—and Santi looked beautiful together. Like a match made in GQ heaven.

With him around, there was no way that I'd ever have a chance with Santi. Yes, he'd called me his boyfriend, but maybe he'd confused his feelings.

I'd been his support network when his brother wasn't around and his friends were all paired up. It was only natural that he'd get close to the only other single person he knew.

It was totally my fault that I'd fallen for him because I should have known better, so I couldn't even get angry. Not when sadness and heartbreak were the overriding emotions.

The exit door was conveniently located by the restrooms.

I'd apologize to Tom and everyone another day because right then...I just had to get out of there.

SANTI

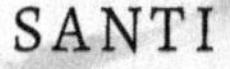
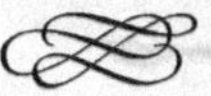

I never thought I'd be so relieved to see Zeke's smug face.

As soon as Mrs. Rosenberg lifted her paddle for the first time, she was one hundred percent determination and one thousand percent scary.

Visions of being kept a slave in a basement flooded my mind until my eyes settled on Micah. If I survived this ordeal unscathed, I was going to take him home and make love to him until the sun came up. I was going to tell him how I'd fallen for him so hard and so fast that there was no way back for us.

As the bidding war between Mrs. Rosenberg and Zeke went on, all I could think was that I wanted this to be over as soon as possible.

At least Micah wasn't on his own at the table. I'd kill Indy and Tate another time for leaving my man, but I was glad to see him in Charlie and Kris's company.

Next to me, Tom was so excited, he was practically vibrating.

When Mrs. Rosenberg finally gave up the fight, I was so

relieved, I couldn't help but hug Zeke tight when he came over to the stage.

"Dude, what the fuck are you doing here?" I asked.

"It looked like you needed to be rescued from the crazy lady with the bright-red nails."

"Don't even. My balls are so far up, I can feel them in my throat. I don't even know how to thank you."

"Does that mean you'll put out now?" he said into my ear.

I laughed. "What will your new boyfriend have to say about that?"

"You can ask him when you move to Lydovia," he said with a wink.

I shook my head. "Not a chance, man. Everything I need is right here." Except, when I looked at the table, Micah wasn't there. "Come on, I need to find the reason I'm not moving and introduce him to you."

Zeke's face was priceless, which made me laugh even more. I dragged him over to the table where Kris and Charlie were engrossed in conversation.

Charlie was the first one to look up. "Nice show, guys."

"Where's Micah?" I asked.

"Oh, I think he went to the restroom," Charlie said.

Zeke and I sat down, and I filled a glass with champagne. Maybe the bubbles would calm me down after the traumatic experience of the auction.

"So, tell me—" Zeke and I said at the same time.

"You first," he said.

"Tell me about this boyfriend of yours. Luca said you're pretty serious about him."

Zeke's face went from his normal chill to hearts appearing in his eyes.

"Istvan is...I don't know. He puts up with me like no

one else ever has. It seems nothing I do phases him. He's the most chill guy I've ever met. I kinda needed that in my life, I just didn't know it until I met him."

"So you're not mad that we never hooked up? I know I kinda left you hanging, but I liked you too much to make it weird if we had," I said.

"Wait," Charlie interrupted. "You mean you guys never..."

Zeke and I shook our heads.

"But you did that whole prank, and then Zeke was naked..." Charlie said, looking at us like he now saw us in a totally different light.

"Man, that was fun," Zeke said. "But my streaking days are over. Istvan is the only one with access to my carefully crafted body. How about you, Santi?"

I laughed. "I was never caught streaking, so technically, it never happened."

"I'm talking about your man. Who is he?"

"You have a new man?" Charlie asked with interest. "Man, why do I never get the gossip first?"

"Because in this place, you blink, and someone's in love, married, and with a kid on the way," Indy said as he and Tate returned to the table.

They were sporting ear-to-ear smiles, but not the kind you get from a quick orgasm.

"Hold on...love, marriage, kid...are you saying...?" I leaned over the table, my gaze flicking between both men as they looked at each other.

"We didn't want to say anything until it was official. We're going to be parents to a baby boy."

Everyone stood to congratulate Indy and Tate, and for a moment, the only talk at the table was about babies and sleeping patterns.

I looked at my watch. Micah wasn't back from the restroom yet.

"Hey guys, I'm going to check on Micah. He's been gone a while."

"I knew it!" Charlie said, pointing at me. "The way Micah was staring at the stage like he wanted to either strip you or carry you away had to mean something. He did look a little upset when he left, or maybe he wasn't feeling well."

I ran to the men's restroom, only to find it empty. I wanted to check the parking lot, but I couldn't do it on my own, so I went back to the table.

"Zeke, I need your help."

On the way out, I explained everything to Zeke, and I had to hand it to him, he didn't even flinch when I told him I was going blind. He just asked me to describe Micah's car to him.

After twenty minutes of searching every corner of the parking lot, I came to the conclusion that Micah had left. But why? Everything was good with us, wasn't it? We'd even shared some flirty messages before I went up on the stage.

The stage.

Fuck, he'd seen how Zeke and I had greeted each other.

"Zeke, I need to get to him."

"Hold on, let me find out what Luca and Ryan's plans are for tonight."

We walked back into the big manor house while Zeke radioed the guys. Kris and Charlie were staying at the house overnight so they could have breakfast with James and Connor in the morning before they left. Luca and Ryan were staying too.

Luca gave Zeke our spare house keys and told him to

crash there after dropping me off and then come back in the morning.

After giving Zeke the directions to Micah's place, I couldn't face talking, so the drive was silent. The darkness of the car made me completely blind, but rather than that, it was the possibility that Micah was at home feeling rejected and upset that really broke my heart.

I wanted to ask Zeke to put the pedal to the metal to get to Micah faster, but I knew he was likely already going the speed limit.

"Don't worry, man. It'll all be good once he hears you out," he said.

"I know, but what if he doesn't want to hear me out?"

"Then you stand naked on his doorstep until he opens up. If he loves you as much as you love him, he won't want to have anyone else looking at your tight ass. Once you're in, you kiss him until he's ready to listen to you."

I smiled at the typical Zeke reply. "Speaking from experience?"

He laughed. "Yup."

My hands shook as I felt Zeke park the car.

"I'll come up with you," he said.

I got out of the car, and Zeke took my hand and placed it on his arm to guide me.

When we got to the door, I knocked and waited. It felt like a million years before I heard the door unlock, followed by a small gasp and then silence.

"Micah?"

I hated that my eyes were taking their time to adjust, even though there was light in the hallway behind Micah. I could tell that much.

"What are you doing here, Santi? What is he doing

here?" he said. His voice sounded different, more raspy and sad, and I wondered if he'd been crying.

"He's here because I'm fucking blind, and you ran away from me."

"Aren't you meant to be on your date?"

Zeke shifted next to me. "Hi, I'm Zeke. I'd love to get to know you better, but jetlag is getting the best of me, so I need to find a bed stat."

"I'm afraid I can't help you with that. The sanctuary is full at the moment," Micah said.

Zeke and I laughed.

"God, I fucking love you when you're sassy," I said. "Zeke, fuck off now. There's clearly no need for me to get naked out here."

My eyesight was slowly returning, and I could make out Zeke giving me the bird before leaving.

"I saw that," I said.

"No, you didn't," he shouted back.

I turned to Micah and held out my hand. He took it like I knew he would because he was a good person, and even if he was hurting—something I was going to rectify—he still wouldn't leave me helpless outside.

When he closed the door, I pushed him against it, trapping him with my body. I could now see the green in his eyes and the red around them, which meant he'd been crying.

"I'm sorry you cried," I whispered. My mouth was so close to his.

"Why are you here?"

I traced his brows with my finger and then cradled his face, tilting it up so he had no choice but to look into my eyes. It would be the only way he'd believe me.

"I'm here because this is where the man I love is. Why would I want to be elsewhere?"

He gasped. "What? You...you do?"

"I do, baby. So much it scares me. It scares me more than going blind because I can learn to be blind, but I'll never forgive myself if I hurt you."

"But how about Zeke?"

"He's a good friend. Nothing ever happened between us."

"I heard him in the restroom. He said he was going to get you to move to Lydovia, and he said he was going to bid on you."

"He said that because he didn't know I already have everything I need here. Last Christmas, I wasn't in a good place. I'd just been diagnosed and was dealing with it on my own. Zeke was a distraction, but we never even kissed, let alone more. He bid on me for a laugh, but once he saw Mrs. Rosenberg's intentions, he did it to help me. He's in a relationship and very happy."

Micah let out a long breath as if he were releasing all the tension he'd been carrying.

"I love you too. That's why I left. I couldn't bear to see you with someone else. I'm sorry I let my insecurities get the best of me again. I just...after overhearing the conversation and then seeing how much he was willing to bid for you, I assumed whatever was going on between you was stronger than what we have."

I pulled him into my arms and held him tight. We were still by the front door that had direct access to his apartment.

"You don't need to apologize. I probably would have reached the same conclusion you did if I was faced with the same situation. In fact..."

"What..."

I pulled away to look at him again. "That day we went to the beach? I was jealous of your friend."

"Who? Spence?"

I shrugged. "Is he the one with the beach house?"

Micah nodded.

"Then he's the one. I wondered what kind of friendship you had. If you went to college together, I worried your relationship was stronger than ours."

"He's straight. Just so you know," Micah said.

"I don't care now, and I don't care about Zeke or anything else. You know what I care about?"

Micah shook his head.

"I care about going upstairs and showing you how much you mean to me, how much we belong together. Are you up for that, baby?"

His reply came in the form of a claiming kiss.

Message received. Loud and clear.

MICAH

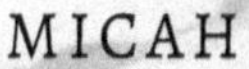

The only way to move on from the misunderstandings, the doubts, and especially my crippling lack of self-confidence was to start afresh.

And the best way to do that was by claiming Santi's mouth.

He responded by pushing me back against the door, trapping me with his big body.

I loved being at his mercy. No, I craved it. Being under Santi made me feel like I was in charge, which was strange because, in some ways, he had all the power. But when he was so close to losing it, that power was transferred to me. Because I'd made him that way.

"Santi..."

"Hmm, Micah..."

He ground his hips, and I felt his erection against my belly. I needed more. And less. More of Santi. Fewer clothes.

I put my hand over his mouth to get his attention. He only pushed it against me, licking and kissing my palm as if he was doing it to my mouth.

"Fuck, Santi...stop. I need to ask you something."

"What's that?"

"I want you to fuck me." I opened my eyes wide, not believing I'd just voiced what I'd wanted for so long.

"No."

What?

"Oh, sorry, I didn't realize. I thought you liked to switch. That's okay, let's go to the bedroom."

I tried to move, but he pinned me back.

"I *am* versatile," he rasped. "But I won't fuck you. I want to fucking make love to you."

I smiled and bit my lip. "Then what are we doing all the way down here?"

He bent his legs and picked me up before carrying me to the bedroom like he'd done before.

"God, I love how easily you can manhandle me," I said.

"You think you're bigger than you actually are, but I'll carry you for as long as I can, and even when I can't see where I'm going, I'll still carry you while you direct me."

"Fuck, stop saying things that make me love you more," I groaned, but I didn't mean it, and he knew I didn't either.

"Nope. That would be detrimental to my life goals."

I laughed. "And what are those?"

"Making sure you love me so much that you'll let me keep you forever."

He laid me on the bed and pulled my shirt off as well as my pajama pants and underwear.

"Forever is a long time. You sure you want me for that long?"

He raised my arms over my head and inhaled all the way down until he buried his face in my armpit. "Oh yeah, a million percent. Hell yeah."

"Then show me, Santi. Show me how much you love me."

"With pleasure."

The promise I'd made him earlier in my message to lick him from head to toe was reversed. He was the one worshiping my skin as if I were the best ice cream he'd ever had.

When my body was vibrating with need, he finally grabbed the lube and condom from the side table.

"I'm prepped," I blurted out.

"What?"

I covered my face, but Santi moved my hands so I had no choice but to look at him.

"How come you're prepped, Micah?"

"Um...well...I wouldn't say I'm prepped *prepped*, but I helped things along earlier because I was going to ask you to fu—make love to me tonight."

Santi's eyes went impossibly dark and his voice a few decibels lower. "Tell me what you did, Micah."

"I douched, and then I used a plug that I thought would be close to your size." I was absolutely sure I was going to die of embarrassment, but Santi looked like he would fuck me right now if we didn't have to do silly things like put condoms on and get lubed up.

"I wanted to savor you, baby, but you're making me so horny with the image of you walking around with a plug in your ass just for me."

He removed his clothes, not caring that the suit he wore was bespoke or how much it had cost him. In five seconds, he was naked, with his long cock pointing to its destination as he lowered himself over my body.

I canted my hips to get some friction on my cock and gasped when I felt his hard dick.

"Fuck, I can't wait to feel you inside me, stretching me."

"I love your dirty mouth, baby."

"And I love you, now, please...I need you."

He sucked the skin of my neck to the point I knew I'd have a hickey or three. "So demanding."

"I've been waiting for this for a long time."

I moaned my relief when, instead of playing with my already too-hard cock, or drawing out foreplay, he sat on his heels and put the condom on.

When he added lube to his finger and ran it over my hole, I tensed up.

I didn't mean to. God knew I'd been looking forward to this for what seemed like a lifetime, and we were almost to the point of no return.

"It's okay, baby. We're not rushing this, no matter how impatient you are."

He kissed me until I couldn't remember my name, and I was rubbing against him like a dog in heat.

"No," I groaned when he moved away from me, but it was only so he could lay on the bed with me straddling him.

"Use your fingers, Micah. Do what you know feels good to you, and when you're ready, take the lead."

I could have cried because that was exactly what I needed. After years of bringing myself to climax and getting to know my body and what I liked, it was daunting putting all that trust in someone else.

Not that I didn't trust Santi. I trusted him with my life. But my body just needed to adjust to this part.

I grabbed the bottle of lube and spread some on my fingers before reaching behind me to seek my hole.

I circled the rim, pressing against my hole enough to feel good but not taking it further.

Santi sat up and started licking and sucking any skin he

could reach in his current position. I moaned when I pushed the first finger through the ring of muscle, and he put his hand over mine, feeling for what I was doing.

"Next time, I want to watch this because you're so fucking sexy right now," he said.

"Ugnh..." The second and third fingers took a little longer, but soon I was fucking my own fingers and delighting in Santi's hand there, just pressing against mine.

I didn't realize I had my eyes closed until Santi added one of his fingers, and I opened them.

"Fuck, Micah, I can't wait to be inside you."

"Now...please, now..."

I removed my fingers and lined up his cock with my hole. He put his hands on my hips but otherwise lay still, waiting for me to take my time.

After such thorough prep, I hoped I could take him all the way in.

I locked my gaze with his and watched the tendons on his neck tense as I lowered myself onto him slowly.

There was still some pain, but nothing I wasn't used to. The difference was that Santi's cock wasn't made of silicone or glass. It was rigid and warm, and I could feel it pulsing inside me as he enjoyed the tightness of my channel around him.

"Jesus, Micah, that feels...argh...too good."

I didn't speak until I was fully seated and ready to move.

"This would be a good time for you to manhandle me and fuck me into the mattress," I said.

He kissed me hard and then put one arm around my waist, turning us over so his body was covering mine.

I may or may not have blissfully sighed my satisfaction at feeling his strong, heavy body over mine.

"I told you, I'm not fucking you. We're making love...
we're just gonna make love hard."

"Potayto, potaaaahh!" I shouted when he pulled back
and slammed right in. And then he did it again and again
until there were stars in my eyes and the rest of the world
ceased to exist.

"Fuck, Santi, you're gonna make me come." My orgasm
was right there beneath the surface, ready to rock my world.

"Do it, come on my dick."

He didn't need to ask twice. I reached for my cock, and
with a couple of strokes, I was coming.

Santi never stopped moving. My orgasm dragged on
forever until he came with a roar.

"Micah!"

We lay chest to chest, too out of breath to kiss.

I winced a little when he pulled out, but it was the
perfect reminder of what we'd just done.

Some people might say you lose your virginity when
you're penetrated for the first time, but I'd disagree. You can
be penetrated by toys, fingers, and a number of other
objects. That doesn't mean you've lost your virginity. It just
means you've found the right buttons in your body to bring
it pleasure.

The day I lost my virginity was the day I gave my body
to Santi for the first time. The rest was just another step in
our intimacy journey.

"Shower?" he asked.

"Absolutely."

We washed each other slowly. It had been a long night,
and I'd need to catch up with our friends in the morning,
but for now, it was time for lazy kisses and falling asleep
wrapped against the man I loved.

I was no longer embarrassed about being naked around

Santi, so once I dried myself, I hung up the towel and pulled his hand toward the bedroom.

"What the hell?"

Santi bumped into my back when I stopped abruptly. He looked over my shoulder and cursed.

Olive, Gus, Alfie, and Doug were all on the bed, staring at us as if daring us to tell them to leave. On the frame of the bed was George, the cursing parrot.

"Fuck. Fuck. Oh, Micah. Yeah. Fuck. Just like that. Cock," the parrot mimicked.

Santi groaned. "We are not adopting another pet."

"You should have thought of that before having sex within earshot of a cursing parrot."

THREE MONTHS LATER

"*B*aby..." I called softly into Micah's ear.

"Hmm...shh, go away."

I smiled and kissed the back of his neck.

"Who are you? Go away. I sleep."

"I'm just one of the many creatures on your bed. Seriously, we need to talk about this."

He moaned and turned around.

"They're not waking me up, you are. So I vote they stay."

I laughed and pressed my mouth against his, sucking his lip and then his tongue until he was grinding against me.

"Still want me gone?" I asked.

"Hmm, I guess not." He opened his eyes. "Morning."

"Morning, baby."

"Good morning. Fuck. Micah. Ooh fuck."

"George!" we both shouted at the bird, and Olive raised her head, growling at us for telling her precious friend off.

"Didn't you close the door last night?" he asked.

"Yup. They work as a team, so we're outnumbered."

Micah groaned and got up.

We worked around each other to use the bathroom and get ready for the day.

Apart from the week my brother had come back for the bachelor event, I hadn't spent a single night away from Micah since that first night. And if it were up to us, that would never happen.

I now understood the smooshy face I always saw on my brother and Ryan. I'd always hoped they'd end up together because I knew they were meant to be almost from the moment they met, but I never thought it was something I'd have.

At first because I didn't think my military career was conducive to a healthy and stable relationship, and then it was because of my eyesight. I was wrong on both accounts.

Many of my men had long-lasting relationships, and they were still in the military, which proved my belief wrong. And my eyesight had never been a factor in the way Micah fell in love with me. He simply just did. Maybe it was my charming personality, or maybe he just felt I needed saving from all the pets that claimed me as theirs.

We had breakfast together, and then I walked down to the clinic with him.

He was only working through the morning because the grand opening of the Chester Falls Animal Sanctuary and Educational Farm was in the afternoon.

It was a mouthful of a name, but it was important to Micah that people knew exactly what he did. The funds raised at the bachelor's ball helped Micah finish the barn, so he was able to comfortably house a number of animals.

When Micah told me about his idea of a petting farm that could host school trips and teach kids about both pets and farm animals, I thought it would be a great success.

The funds just about covered it all, which meant Micah could afford the finishing touches.

"What time's your class?" he asked, wrapping his arms around my waist.

"In half an hour. Long enough for me to walk there."

"You're sure you don't want me to drop you off?"

"I'm sure. I think this is something I need to do on my own."

My eyesight hadn't deteriorated much since my diagnosis. But at night, I was completely blind, which meant we either had to have a lot of lights on or make some adjustments so there were clear paths everywhere I needed to go inside the apartment.

I insisted on the latter. I wanted to embrace my condition rather than fight it because it helped me focus on what was really important.

There were still times when I became extremely frustrated, but Micah and I worked through it together.

Today I was going to my first braille class. It was the first big step toward my goal of going back to school to train to be a coach. It was my biggest strength and what I'd loved the most in the military.

Before I was discharged, I'd considered applying for a training job, but I'd been too focused at the time on a different part of my career. Now, I was looking forward to helping people find their own strengths and achieve their goals.

"Okay, be safe out there. Is Olive going with you?" Micah asked.

"Yes, and we've already had the conversation. No one else is coming."

"Did she sulk?"

"Yup."

He shook his head. "I'm a vet, and even I know that isn't normal behavior for pets."

"Meh. We're all perfect as we are. Our own weird and slightly dysfunctional family."

I kissed him gently, knowing I couldn't get carried away. We were bound to be interrupted by April.

"Speaking of family..." Micah said.

I sighed.

Micah had met my parents a few times because they were only in New Haven, but I hadn't met his parents other than over video call. Interestingly enough, our parents knew each other, which was a good thing...I hoped.

"If it's out, I can touch it, so make sure you cover up your glitter guns."

Micah laughed but didn't move, so neither did I.

"Morning, Tom, what brings you so early? And how did you get past April?" I asked.

He winked. "One happy brownie and a wedding invite."

"In that order?" Micah asked.

Tom's eyes bulged. "God, no. April is lovely, but I've already spread my glitter all over Wren. He'll never get rid of me now. Brownie was for April, and the wedding invite is for you."

He held out a sealed envelope sealed with glittery wax. We wouldn't have expected anything less from Tom.

"Congratulations," I said, taking the envelope. "You can count on us...well, as long as Mrs. Rosenberg isn't invited."

"Don't worry, you're safe. Ciao for now." He waved and left.

"I'm not sure if I should be happy for Wren or plan a rescue mission," I said.

Micah hit my arm. I tightened my hold and bent him over for a kiss. "See you later, baby."

The last school bus had left, so I leaned against the barn wall and took a deep breath.

Our supporters were still around, helping to feed the animals and talking amongst themselves.

The opening of the sanctuary had been a success, and I finally felt worthy of all the work Tom put into the fundraiser and the money raised.

Until I had something to show for it, I'd felt so guilty having all that money. And when there had been a few delays, I'd been really stressed. Santi kept telling me not to worry, but I couldn't. It was in my nature to worry.

"So this is where you're hiding."

Santi approached with the whole family on his heel and George sitting on his shoulder.

"Ooh, pretty dick, pretty dick."

"Jesus Christ," I said. "Thank god the kids are all gone."

"George, we can't take you anywhere, you know that?" I said, rubbing his feathers.

"Take me, take me. Ooh fuck."

A few heads turned our way, so I pulled Santi by his shirt to follow me.

"Where are we going?" he asked.

"You mean apart from going away from everyone because of George?"

He snorted.

"I want to show you something."

We walked to the far end of the field, where I'd found some markings.

"Oh, what's this?" Santi asked.

"My guess is Grandad wanted to build something here, and these stones are painted to delineate the outline of whatever it was. Maybe this is where he dreamed of building his sanctuary. I was thinking..." I paused to look at Santi. "Maybe we could build a house here. For us and the pets. Nothing fancy, but all on one level with a wraparound porch that we could sit and enjoy the sunset warming our faces at the end of the day."

He looked around to take everything in. "I think that's a great idea. I'm sure we can save up while we think about what we want."

The back of my neck was so hot I was pretty sure Santi could see the change of color.

"Um...you see...Grandad knew I was like him. I love animals, and I'd do anything to help an animal in need. So he did something in the trust he left me to make sure I wouldn't forget to look after myself too."

"What did he do?"

"He put in a clause that part of the trust fund could only be used to buy or build a house for me to live in."

Santi was rooted in place. "Are you...is this for real?"

I nodded, feeling the rest of my body heat up. "I was also wondering...fuck, this is hard. Santi...I was hoping you'd marry me so we can move into our new house together as a married couple. I think things happen in life for a reason. And for whatever reason, I didn't have sex or even a relationship with anyone until I met you. Waiting so long for us makes me appreciate our relationship even more, but it doesn't mean we need to do everything slowly. In fact, I'd love it if we didn't wait that long because there's no point in waiting when you know who you're going to spend the rest of your life with."

Santi's Adam's apple bobbed up and down, and he bit his lip. He stared at me until a tear fell down his cheek.

I crossed the space between us and hugged him, making George move to perch on something, or someone, else.

"I love you so much, Santi. And I know you love me. We make each other stronger even when we drive each other mad. Marry me?"

He held me tight, and I felt his nod against my neck. "Yes. Yes, Micah, I'll marry you. Tomorrow if you want."

I laughed, but it came out funny because of my relief that he'd said yes.

"Let's wait till after Tom and Wren's wedding. Maybe until the house is ready. It can be our honeymoon house. We can even have a naked-only policy," I said.

"Only if George doesn't move in. The last thing we need is for him to start singing *big dick, big dick*."

I laughed so hard I nearly cried. "Big dick, huh?"

"You know it, baby."

I did know it. I knew that the past didn't define our future. I knew that the people in our past could still hurt us in the present but could also be the ones who saved us.

I knew that just like Charlie caught his prince, Tom caught his rival, Connor caught his bodyguard, Indy caught his bachelor, and Aiden caught his biker, so had I caught my own sexy vet.

~

Thank you so much for reading *How to Catch a Vet*, the sixth book in the Chester Falls series. Keep reading to get two special bonus scenes.

Up next is *How to Catch a Happy Ever After*. This is the final book in the Chester Falls series. Revisit your favorite couples one last time. And whose turn will it be to have their own Happy Ever After? Maybe those who you will least expect.

Be sure to follow me on Bookbub to be notified of new releases, and look for me on Facebook for sneak peaks of upcoming stories.

Please take a moment to write a review of *How to Catch a Vet*. If you leave a review Micah will let you spend a full day at his Sanctuary where you'll get to pet all the animals. Honest!

If you would like to be the first to know when my new releases are available, read exclusive FREE stories and know what I'm up to, please sign up for my newsletter, Ana's VIP Readers: *bit.ly/AnaAshley*.

For giveaways, sneak peaks, ARC opportunities and general caffeinated fun times, please join my facebook group! Café RoMMance - Ana's Reader Group.

DROWNING THE VOICES TOGETHER

SANTI

"Red velvet or gold? Maybe both and add a little green? And sparkles?" Tom flicked the giant book with fabric samples taking up most of the table at Spilled Beans. Hard enough that I had to hold my coffee in my hand, or I'd risk it spilling everywhere. Let's not mention how he stress-ate my muffin and didn't even realize it. His hair was messy from how much he'd run his hands through it.

"Are you really asking for color advice from a blind guy?" I asked.

"Desperate times call for desperate measures. Everyone is busy, and you're not totally blind, so suck it up, buttercup, and help me out."

I snorted. What he meant was that everyone was avoiding him like the plague.

"Tom, I'm a military man. What the heck do I know about colors?"

"Have you looked at your boyfriend?" he asked.

"Fiancé," I corrected.

He did a double take and smiled wide before shaking his head as if to return to his original thought. "Have you looked at your...fiancé?"

"Not enough times, in my opinion," I said, pressing the button on my watch that read the time into my earpiece.

Even though my vision wasn't totally gone, I was trying to adjust to living as a legally blind person and making the best of the technology available. A good buddy from special forces had customized a smartwatch to connect to an almost invisible earpiece. It helped me get my bearings when needed by giving me information such as the time, directions, the name of anyone calling my phone, and many other functions I was still testing.

The piece allowed me to still hear my surroundings. Even though Olive wasn't a guide dog, she'd become my shadow, and I trusted her instincts when we were out. Between Olive and my technology, I felt comfortable going out on my own, regardless of how bright or dark it was outside.

"And what is your point?" I asked, wondering where Tom's line of questioning was going.

"You clearly have good taste in men because Micah is H-O-T, so stop moaning and help me out."

I had no clue about the relationship between good taste in men and knowing anything about coordinating colors, but I didn't care when I was saved by the sex-on-legs hot vet walking into Spilled Beans. As if she was clearly not enjoying the conversation she was witnessing, Olive took off toward the door to greet Micah, who crouched to let her have some cuddles. I was happy to wait for mine.

"Why is Wren marrying you?" I asked.

"Huh? What do you mean? Do you think he doesn't

want to marry me? Have you been talking to him? Oh shit, I drove him away with too much wedding talk." Tom's violet eyes reddened and his breathing became labored.

"Hey, calm down. That's not what I meant. Wren is crazy about you, and you know it. What I meant is that he's marrying you because he loves you. He won't care if your color scheme is black. I guarantee he will still be at the altar waiting for you."

Tom's shoulders sagged. "I want this to be perfect. Somehow, I can't use my own magic on myself. No one told me that was a condition of having my powers."

I laughed, my breath catching when my eyes met Micah's and I saw the smile he reserved only for me.

I used to think the worst part of going blind was that one day I would no longer be able to see his smile, but then he taught me I didn't need my eyes to see or feel it.

"Tom," I said, closing his big book of fabrics and putting my hands on his, "this is yours and Wren's day. When you think of you two as a couple, how does it feel?"

His smile returned alongside a look I knew well because I felt it too. "We're strong together, invincible. We're the days of football practice and the nights of lovemaking. We're the calm in the storm and the rainbow at the end. We shine like the sun and sparkle like the stars."

I looked around, and everyone was staring at Tom. I squeezed his hand.

"I think you've just written your vows. Something tells me finding your color won't be a problem."

He stared at me as if he'd just realized what he'd said.

"By the way, you owe me a muffin." I stood and walked to the man who was my sun, stars, and everything in between.

Micah stood and put his arms around my waist. "Hey."

"Hey, beautiful." I pressed my lips against his briefly, congratulating myself for not mauling him in the middle of Indy's coffee shop. "Ready to go home?"

He nodded. I paid Indy for my coffee and the box of pastries he was holding for me behind the counter, and with Olive beside me, we walked out into the afternoon sun.

We walked home in silence. I kept my eyes closed under my sunglasses and listened to all the noises from the road. How far people were and which direction the cars came from. Much like sitting in Spilled Beans, this was another exercise in developing my hearing, and I knew neither Micah nor Pickles would let me walk into incoming traffic.

I figured we were closer to home from the change in the scent. So many of the houses near Micah's clinic had gardens with rose bushes. It always smelled wonderful, and I was looking forward to discovering if it changed in the winter.

Olive picked up her pace. Which meant we were really close, and she cared less about me and more about getting home to her friends. I opened my eyes slowly and let them adjust to the light.

As usual, my eyes sought Micah, but what I found when I looked at him wasn't what I was hoping to see.

"Is everything okay, sweetheart?" I asked, pulling him closer to me, even though we were only a few feet away from the side door leading straight to our apartment above the clinic.

"Yeah, sure."

I didn't press him for answers because I wanted to get him inside first, but there was no way I'd let it rest. He was clearly upset over something, and I needed to know what it was so I could fix it.

"Fuck. Cock. Yah, fuck it. Fuck it all."

We groaned at George's greeting as soon as we opened the door. He was perched on the banister, and when Olive squished her way past us, he flew to get a doggy lift upstairs.

"Is there an etiquette class we can send him to?" I asked.

Micah shrugged as he locked the door behind us.

I took the stairs and went straight to our bedroom, ignoring the pets sleeping in Olive's bed, including Gus.

I turned the water on to fill the bathtub and placed the pastry box on the shelf above the taps. After squirting a good amount of bubble bath, I left the water running and went back out.

Micah was in the bedroom, removing his shoes, lost in thought.

"Will you tell me what's upsetting you, baby?" I put my arms around him from behind and started unbuttoning his shirt.

His arms fell to the side as he took a deep breath and let me undress him. I placed small kisses on his neck and shoulders as I removed his shirt and then turned him around.

"It's nothing, really. Just stuff in my head," he said.

I cradled his face, feeling his wiry but soft beard under my thumbs.

"Have I told you today how beautiful you are?" I asked.

He nodded.

"Have I told you today how much I love you?"

He nodded again, his lip trembling a little.

"Come with me." I took his hand and pulled him into the bathroom, where the water in the tub was at the perfect level. I turned the taps off and got undressed.

My reaction to being near Micah was as usual: rock hard and pure need.

It seemed my body spoke louder than my words because

Micah took the rest of his clothes off, and I watched as his cock hardened in reaction to mine.

He took my hands and placed them on his face like he did whenever he wanted me to really see him.

"Today, I let the ugly voices of my past get through and tell me I'm not good enough. That I am ugly, fat, and worthless—"

"Micah..."

He kissed my palms as I ran my fingers over his eyes, soft lips, and beard.

"I know they're wrong, Santi. I know I'm not any of those things...but will you show me?"

My ultimate life goal was to make sure Micah was happy and never felt insecure again, so I could absolutely do that and more, and not entirely for selfless reasons.

Confident Micah turned me on like nothing else. Confident Micah was bossy and sassy, and he owned me, heart and soul.

I settled in the tub and pulled him to rest against my chest. My cock was hard and poking his back. But it was okay because this wasn't about me. I'd still take my pleasure, but Micah was first.

I grabbed the sponge and dipped it in the soapy water. Then I ran it over his chest until he was all wet and slippery.

When I reached under the water for his cock, he exhaled and leaned his head back over my shoulder.

"That's it, baby. Just feel and let me take care of you."

I dropped the sponge in the water and used my left hand to touch Micah everywhere I could reach while my right hand stroked him the way I knew drove him crazy.

"Argh, Santi." He moaned and trembled under my touch.

My cock wasn't even neglected because it was deliciously trapped between us, and the way he was moving against me had me close to coming.

"Look at you, baby. So beautiful. I love when you give yourself to me. When you trust me to look after you. Fuck, Micah, I love you so much. Please never forget it. Never let the voices tell you otherwise."

He shook his head. His moans got louder and water sloshed around us as he got closer to his orgasm.

I opened my legs wider and tugged his balls while my fingers sought his hole. He seemed happy to take my fingers in, but I wouldn't do it. Not without proper prep.

What wouldn't I do for the chance to see what was happening under the water. His hole relaxed around my fingers, needing more.

"There's enough soap, Santi. Please, I need it."

I couldn't say no to him, but I took it slow. In this position, it would be hard to reach his prostate, so I kept a slow pace, thrusting the tip of my middle finger in and out of his hole.

"Oh fuck, Santi. Feels so good."

"That's it, baby. Come for me. Let go. I'll be here to catch you."

I didn't care that water was everywhere on the floor by the bathtub. I'd clean it all on my hands and knees just for the pleasure of seeing Micah come apart like this.

He finally let go on a string of curses, and I only spared a thought for the cursing parrot in the living room before the pressure in my balls became too much. I stroked myself to orgasm, coming against Micah's back.

I leaned my head against the wall, savoring Micah's soft body, now a lot more relaxed.

He turned his head, and I caught his lips in a searing kiss.

"Who do you hear now?" I asked, running my hand over his beard.

"Only you, Santi. Only you."

"You want to tell me what happened?"

He turned away again but leaned back against me.

"I walked past a group of kids and heard their conversation. It's ridiculous but hearing them talk about another kid got to me. I always knew when people talked about me. Even when I didn't overhear the conversations, their looks, the sniggers, and the hands covering their smiles as I walked past didn't hide what they were saying or thinking."

"Do you know which kid they were talking about? Maybe we can talk to Wren," I asked.

"No. They didn't mention a name."

"When I joined the army, I thought everyone needed to be big and strong to make it there. I was wrong. The medics, IT personnel, intelligence. A strong, efficient team needs different people to succeed. Everyone's important... Maybe I can talk to Wren and the high school principal and do a talk for the kids. I'll invite them to speak to me if they want to know more. That should send a clear message to the kids talking shit about other kids."

Micah was silent for a while, so I wondered if I'd overstepped with my intentions.

"Thank you. You have no idea how much that means to me."

I held him tight. "I do, baby. Trust me. I do."

The bathroom door slammed open, and suddenly, we were invaded.

George flew in and perched on the towel rail, which, fortunately, wasn't heated.

"I like it. I like it. Love you."

We both laughed.

"That was the tamest sentence he's ever said. Maybe there's still hope," Micah said.

"Fuck me, Santi," George said.

"Nah. It's hopeless. We'll need an annex in the new house just for him and his bad influence."

Micah laughed.

Olive sat next to the tub, resting her head on the edge to ask for ear scratches. Gus chased Alfie around, and Doug was licking the soapy water from the floor.

"I guess we're lucky this time that they waited until we finished," I said. "It's not easy to concentrate on reading braille when you have blue balls."

"Is that because your hands have to be on the book?" he asked.

I nodded.

"Santi?"

"Yeah?"

"I can't wait to marry you, and I can't wait until we move into our new house."

I squeezed him tight. "Ditto, baby. Now, how about we stay here and eat as many of those pastries as possible."

"Sounds like a balanced and wholesome life choice."

I sucked his earlobe, and he groaned but reached for the box.

We were pruny by the time we finished, but I couldn't think of a single thing that would have made the evening better than being with my man, surrounded by our weird but loyal pet family.

BONUS SCENE 2

HOW TO GIFT A VET

SANTI

The closer we got to the clinic's back door, the more Olive pulled on her lead.

"Calm down, girl. I want to see him as bad as you, but if I trip, you'll only be upset with yourself." She growled her disagreement but slowed down.

We were getting a path from our house to the clinic to make it easier for us to go between the two without getting our shoes too muddy, especially during the rainy months.

The past spring had been particularly wet, and considering the menagerie of pets that followed us around, Micah's idea had no contest from me. Especially when he was the one who often ended up cleaning the floors.

Not that I couldn't do it. Case in point, I'd just done it after Olive ran outside and came back soaking wet while I was on a call with a client. Fortunately, she remained self-contained in the mudroom, so after I cleaned her up, I spent some time on my hands and knees, ensuring I got all the dirt from the tiled floor before it dried out.

It was just that Micah worked long hours at the clinic and usually felt bad that I did a lot of our housework. I didn't mind, but I'd do anything to make him happy, so we compromised on the floors because those were harder for me to see.

"Okay, Olive, no snitching," I said, opening the back door.

As soon as we were inside, she ran up the stairs to Micah's old apartment, where the other pets hung out while Micah and I were at work.

I hung my coat by the door and went through to Micah's consultation room. The layout of the old house made it easy to hear if he was with a patient.

There was no sound, so I opened the door. "Babe?"

No reply. As my eyes adjusted to the darker lighting, I could finally see Micah wasn't there. The door to the reception area was open, so I followed the animated voices coming from the other side.

"My grandson designed them. He's very talented, you know?"

I recognized Ethel's voice immediately. She was a sweet, if slightly crazy, old lady who owned three cats. I knew Micah often treated her pets without charging her because Ethel had a small pension, and her husband had died many years ago, leaving her with just the house they lived in.

"Ethel, this isn't what you think it is," Micah said with a tinge of exasperation.

"I told you, Doctor. This is an artistic interpretation of fish. My grandson goes to that fancy art school in Boston."

Micah's sigh couldn't be more audible. Or maybe I was just so attuned to him I could read his moods.

"I saw the drawings in that book he keeps in his bedroom when I visited my son last month," Ethel continued. "Oh, hello, Santi. How are you, dear? Maybe you can settle something for us."

With my presence given away, I took the few remaining steps to stand next to Micah.

He wasn't keen on public displays of affection while working, so I placed my hand on his lower back, which I knew was a safe place. He leaned into my touch, making my heart soar.

"How can I help, Ethel?"

"Well," she said, "I crocheted these beautiful fish. I know Doctor Sawyer doesn't always charge for his services, so I want him to sell these here. It's my way of repaying his kindness."

"Fish?"

"Ethel, these aren't..." Micah stopped with a sigh.

"They are fish," Ethel insisted. "They're cat toys. I just know they'll be wildly popular with your customers."

It didn't sound like a totally bad idea. After all, if it kept Ethel busy, and they made Micah some money, I couldn't see where the issue was. Didn't cats like to play with things? And they liked fish, right?

"Babe, where are these fish? Can I see them?" I asked.

He leaned over the reception desk to retrieve it, placing the toy in my hand. I felt for the shape and texture. I tried to do this before I confirmed with my limited sight that I was right.

"This feels a lot like a bu—"

"Shh, don't say it. It makes it true," Micah whispered.

I snorted. I confirmed my suspicions when I looked at the supposed fish.

Well, Ethel was right. It *was* a toy.

Micah elbowed me, but I couldn't stop the laughter

that bubbled out of me at the thought of Micah selling tiny crocheted butt plugs with smiley faces.

"Look, this one has a hat," Ethel said, handing it over.

After the fourth *fish,* I couldn't see because of the tears, and I couldn't breathe from laughing.

"I tell you what, Ethel. I'll buy them from you. Our pets are going to love them," I said.

"Nonsense. You can keep those. I have a ton more at home. I like to keep my hands busy when I'm watching *Jeopardy.*"

Ethel seemed to consider the matter closed because she grabbed her purse from the reception desk and left.

"Oh, baby," I said, turning Micah to face me.

"You're in the doghouse," he said, pointing a finger at my chest.

I leaned over and pressed my lips against his. He sighed and leaned into the kiss, not resisting when I licked the seam of his lips for a taste of my beautiful husband.

"You're still in the doghouse." He pulled me closer, his hands going round the small of my back and inching closer to my butt the longer we kissed.

When I was seconds away from lifting Micah onto the desk and taking what I wanted, he put some space between us.

"Christ, Santi," he puffed out. "What have I told you repeatedly?"

I chuckled. "Just because I can't see people doesn't mean they can't see me."

"And..."

"The reception area isn't a good place for blowjobs, no matter how much we both want it."

He coughed.

"Fine. No matter how much *I* want it."

"Good."

He locked the front door and grabbed the tiny butt plugs off the desk.

"If you can have the butt plugs, I can keep the donkey," he said.

I followed him to the back of the house via his consultation room.

"I'm sorry, baby. What did you just say?"

"Exactly what you heard," he said. His tone was full of defiance, as if I'd ever deny him anything.

"You want...a donkey? We already have Steve." My watch buzzed. "Come on," I said. "Dinner is ready. We can discuss this new acquisition over food."

Micah held my hand as we walked back out, closing the door behind us. We'd return for the pets once we had our alone time.

It was the only way a guy could have sex without a play-by-play from our pet parrot, George. I loved the feathery dude, but I didn't need to be told what to do to bring pleasure to my husband.

"Wait." I stopped a third of the way to the house, pulling him closer. "You're too quiet..."

"Me? Noo...I'm not quiet. What's for dinner?"

"Nice deflection, baby. Shall I use my special interrogation skills on you later?"

His body trembled against mine. "Yes." His breathy voice made me consider the merits of having dinner later... much later.

Micah didn't notice the clean floor in the mudroom or that I'd changed the washable rug, going straight to the kitchen instead. He opened the oven where the lasagna I'd prepared during my lunch break was now ready to eat.

"This smells amazing, Santi. Thank you," he said,

taking the hot tray out and placing it on top of the stove to cool down.

"Shower," I growled in his ear.

Micah usually showered in his old apartment unless I was home and we took one together. If I wasn't so hungry, I'd have run a bath, but I'd skipped lunch to prepare dinner and had little more than a few cups of coffee and a snack between my calls.

We dropped our clothes in the laundry room and went into our room, naked and ready to play.

"Hey," he complained as I slapped his bare ass.

"You can't jiggle it in front of me and expect no reaction, baby. Your ass is delectable."

I turned the water in the shower on, feeling for the right temperature.

"Busy day?" he asked, stepping in after me.

"Yeah. But good. I never thought I'd enjoy coaching other people so much. I'm tired, but also not." I knew I didn't need to explain further because Micah got it.

He loved being a vet and looking after animals so much that he'd put everything he had on the line for it.

Micah reached out for the shower soap.

"Uh-uh," I said, taking the bottle from him. I squeezed out a dollop and lathered it between my hands before running them over his chest and down his soft belly.

He was the most beautiful man I'd ever been with. The way he responded to my touch, the way he made me feel like I was the most important person in the world. Micah was perfect in every way.

I stroked his hard cock, keeping my grip loose.

"Santi," he moaned.

I massaged his balls with one hand while the other went

around to his crease, finding the heat between his butt cheeks.

"Keep your hands to yourself," I ordered. "This is about you, not me."

"But—"

"Hands. Down."

He huffed, but when I pushed a lathered finger inside his tight heat, he cried out. His cock jerked in my hand.

"Do you want to come, baby?" I asked, knowing the answer already.

"No, I want you to fuck me." His breathlessness gave away how close he was already. His eyes were closed and his lips parted.

I kissed him and stroked his cock through his release. He fought it, but in the end, I got what I wanted. No one knew how to push my man's buttons like I did, and I lived for it.

"You bastard," he said with no real anger.

I chuckled, kissing and sucking the skin on his neck behind his beard.

"I was only taking the edge off, baby. After dinner, I want you to fuck me into the mattress so hard it'll leave a permanent indentation of my sated body."

Even though he couldn't get hard straight away, the small jerk of his cock against my rock-hard one gave me a thrill of anticipation for later.

"Come on, let's finish this shower so you can convince me it's a good idea to get a donkey."

Micah's moves were slow after his orgasm. While he got dressed, I went to the kitchen to finish setting the table and getting our drinks.

"God, this is so good," Micah moaned after putting a forkful of lasagna in his mouth. I was proud of my efforts.

My mom had helped me make a batch of the sauce when she visited, so all I had to do was cook the beef, add the sauce, and layer it with the pasta sheets.

"Um, so..." Micah said, looking away. "We kind of have another donkey."

We already had a rescue donkey, Steve, whose owner passed away, leaving him unattended and without someone to look after him.

"What do you mean, *we* have another donkey?"

Micah straightened up in his chair. "I got a call from someone who works at a circus. They had an older donkey struggling to keep up with all the traveling. They heard about the sanctuary and wondered if we could give Pepper a new home."

"Pepper?"

"That's his name. It's quite fitting. You'll see when you meet him." Micah's smile talking about the donkey was beyond adorable.

"So what you're saying is that this morning we owned one donkey, and a mere ten hours later, we own two donkeys. You're spending too much time with Olive."

He shrugged. "Donkeys are social animals. Steve was on his own too much. I actually think...I think they're in love."

I laughed. "Come again?"

"Pepper came this morning. I was careful not to do too much too soon, but he seemed comfortable and responded well to the other animals, so I thought I'd introduce him to Steve. You should have seen them. It was love at first sight."

I pushed my chair back and took Micah's hand, pulling him so he ended up on my lap.

"It was love at first sight for me too, baby," I said. Maybe I hadn't known it straight away, but the moment I saw Micah by the riverbank with Olive and Gus over his legs, he was already mine.

"Liar." He wrapped his arms around my shoulders and kissed me.

"How about we go out to feed the kids, make sure they're comfortable, and then come back here for dessert?" I asked, rubbing my face on Micah's soft beard.

"We have dessert?"

"*I* have dessert, baby."

He chuckled. "Let me guess."

I lifted his shirt, licking one of his nipples and then the other, making sure I relayed my message without words.

Micah's moan affirmed he'd received it.

There would be time for late-night ice cream. I'd make sure of it.

But not before I had my way with my husband.

PREVIEW OF HOW TO CATCH A HAPPY EVER AFTER

RORY

It had certainly been more than a few years since I last stood in the center of the Chester Falls town square.

Despite the colder than usual fall, somehow everything was blooming. Proof, if any was needed, that the town had its own magic spell. Or maybe just a really good gardener.

The square, as well as the buildings surrounding it, hadn't changed much. I knew that because I remembered every single time I'd been here. And like most of the locations in the small town, the square held my secrets.

It was here that I had my first hotdog from a street vendor after the book fair when I was eight. My grandad had sworn me to secrecy because if my parents knew about it, they'd definitely forbid our weekly adventures into town.

That was the first secret I kept. Inconsequential, now that I thought about it, but it had a much longer-lasting effect on me.

Secrets existed.

Secrets meant I could do normal things.

Secrets kept me safe.

Until that safety became a gilded prison. A self-imposed retreat from myself. And who do you become when you can't be yourself?

In my case, an ugly, cold person who hurts others.

I shivered in the cold despite my heavy coat. Maybe I was just cold all over, and it had nothing to do with the temperature.

Taking a deep breath, I steeled myself for what I was here to do. I had no real excuse to turn back. Especially since this had been my idea. One that my therapist had encouraged.

I walked toward Fabulize, ignoring anything that might be a distraction, such as the man selling roasted chestnuts on the corner of the square or the street art exhibition from the high school art club students.

The door was closed, but the sign was turned to open. Not surprising, considering how cold it was outside. From the entrance, I could see the store's owner by the counter, drawing on a large notepad.

I pushed the door open, the bell giving away my presence.

"Good morning and welcome to Fabulize. I'm Tom, your new fairy godmother and granter of all your fashion wishes."

His smile warmed me up instantly. I'd heard some stories about Tom from my best friend, Connor, but my imagination didn't come anywhere close to what being in front of him was really like.

His eyes were a strange color that looked almost violet. Were they real? Whatever they were, I couldn't take my eyes off him.

"Are you okay there, sweetie?" he asked.

"Yes...um, I'm sorry, you're just so much more than I

thought." I blew out a long breath. "Sorry, that came out all wrong."

He smiled. "Oh, don't you worry. I've been extra since the day I was born. Besides, you can't wear this outfit without owning your sparkle," he said, running his hands down his waistcoat. It was purple with a gold embroidered pattern that looked like those fancy, old French chandeliers.

I nodded, unsure of what to say, and took the embossed wedding invite from the inner pocket of my coat, setting it down on the counter.

"I'm Rory."

I let my name hang like a curse. Well, it felt like a curse to me most of the time.

Tom stood up straight, and his smile went even wider. Then he came out from behind the counter and hugged me.

What's going on? I'm pretty sure this isn't how this is meant to go down.

"I'm so pleased to finally meet you," he said, releasing me. I missed his warmth immediately. "Connor talks about you all the time. I hope you're back to stay. I know he misses you, and James is one pet adoption away from owning a zoo to make up for it."

I laughed. I missed my best friend too. I guess I never considered that he might miss me too now that he was all loved up and married to his childhood best friend.

"Yes, I'm back. That's um...why I'm here," I said.

Tom nodded as he leaned against the counter.

"I don't know where to start," I continued, but Tom held up his hand.

"Hold on. Let me grab us some brownies and a cocktail."

"Cocktail?"

"Don't worry, it's non-alcoholic. I like to be sugared up for heart-to-hearts."

I did a double-take. "How do you know what I'm here for?"

He shrugged and disappeared behind a heavy curtain, coming back a minute later with a plate stacked with mini brownies and two tall glasses filled with a multicolored drink.

"Take a seat." He pointed to the couch.

I followed him and sat on the opposite side, wondering how this visit had turned completely upside down before I'd even said why I'd come to see him.

"Okay, my dear, tell me why you're here. And I hope it's not to decline the invitation to my wedding because it's no taksies-backsies."

He seemed so serious about it that I wasn't sure how to follow. Because he was wrong. I couldn't go to his wedding. I mean, after all I'd done, how could I?

"You're Charlie's best friend. I know he confided in you about us." I cradled the drink with both my hands to have something to do with them. "I'm really sorry about what happened. I've spoken to Charlie..." A lump formed in my throat as I remembered how easily he'd forgiven me when I really didn't deserve it.

Tom put his hand on mine. "You have nothing to apologize for. Not to me, at least."

"But I do. I know Charlie was alone with my secret until he confided in you. I know...you're still keeping his secret. My secret. I appreciate that more than you know, even if I don't deserve it. That's why I need to apologize to you. After I left Chester Falls, I tried coming back so many times, but each try failed because I didn't know how to handle things. I hadn't forgiven myself, and I wasn't ready to talk to other people. But I'm tired of hiding away. I want to live in the only place that ever felt like home to me. And I want to be able to wave to you on the street, to have you make me a suit for a work event, and to not feel like my past is constantly behind me, waiting to push me over."

Tom took a sip of his drink. "Rory, I only have one question for you."

I nodded.

"Are you still in love with Charlie?"

What?

"No. No. I mean, I love him, but I'm not *in love* with him. He's so happy with Kris, he's fulfilling his dreams, and he's a fucking prince now. A prince!"

Tom laughed. "Yeah, I'll never get used to that. I mean, if anyone was born to wear a tiara, it was me, right? It's a good thing Wren treats me like royalty," he said, shoving a brownie in his mouth in the most unroyal manner ever.

"Sorry," he said with his mouth full. "Can't get crumbs on this outfit, or it'll be a bitch to clean."

I held my drink to my lips. Tom was right, it was very sweet, but it was also the thing I didn't know I needed until I took a sip.

"Wow, this is ridiculously good, Tom. What's in it?"

"Wholesome rainbows and a little bit of fairy dust. It always works wonders on those who need a hug in a cup."

My throat tightened. If only Tom knew how much I needed a hug. Or human contact from someone that truly cared beyond the mutual agreement that our time together would be casual and secret.

Fucking secrets.

"Thank you, Tom. I wasn't sure how to do this, and I certainly don't deserve how easily you've forgiven me."

"Like I said, there's nothing to forgive. If you've made

things right with Charlie, then you've made things right with me. Now, about the wedding..." he said.

"I can't go."

"Can't or won't?"

Neither, I thought. I could go to the wedding. It's not like I had a busy social agenda anymore. I also wanted to go, I just... "Maybe it's a bit too soon. It's one thing to make amends and another to join such an important celebration."

Tom grabbed the plate with the brownies and held it up to me. I couldn't resist taking one. He put the plate back on the small coffee table next to the couch and turned to face me. He suddenly looked serious, and I felt like this was a part of Tom he didn't often let out.

"My dads died when I was only a baby. Most of my life, it was just me and my mom, and then there was Charlie. I never thought my family would turn out to be made up of so many wonderful people. If I'd stayed in Boston instead of moving to Chester Falls, I would never have met Wren. Bottom line is, life is too short to live in the dark. Come to the wedding, have more drinks than you should, eat more than is wise, and be the Rory you want to be. Who knows, you may even find your own prince charming to kiss at midnight. It could be the start of your own happy ever after."

I laughed. "Okay, I'll come to the wedding, but as for the second thing...I doubt it."

"Why's that?"

I looked away. "That would mean I'd need to be out."

"Why aren't you? Sorry," Tom said. "No one should be out before they're ready, but wouldn't you be happier if you could openly be yourself?"

I shrugged. "I almost came out to Connor when we were fifteen, but I got too scared. My parents...they're not...

I don't want to talk about them, but if I'd come out, I'd have lost the little freedom I had, including being able to see Connor. It was easier staying in the closet, and then it was just too late."

Tom stood up and went over to one of his display shelves, coming back a moment later holding a burnt-orange scarf in his hand.

He wrapped it around my neck and then placed a hand-held mirror in front of my face.

"Butterflies start out as larvae, the rainbow starts out as rain. You can come out in your own time, but don't walk out of this door thinking it's too late, Rory, because it's not. Whenever you want to do it, I can guarantee you'll be accepted. I don't know what your family situation is like, but here in Chester Falls, you already have one waiting for you."

I felt my eyes water and had to take a deep breath so I wouldn't cry. God, I was so tired of everything. All I wanted was to bathe in Tom's kind words and believe they were true.

"Thank you, Tom. You have no idea how much this means to me."

"I do, Rory. Trust me, I do. See? You already look like a different person. You can be what you want to be."

The way he said it made me wonder what he meant. It was hard to believe that Tom could be anything else but this kind, sparkly person in front of me. Then again, I knew how ugly the world was out there, so maybe he'd had his fair share of punches thrown his way.

I left the store with a promise to come back to get a suit for the wedding after Tom insisted I keep the scarf.

His words also stayed with me. Could I do it? Could I be an openly gay man?

Tom was right. I would be accepted. After all, Connor thought he was straight all his life until he reconnected with James, and out of all the challenges they'd faced, Connor coming out didn't seem to have been one of them.

The wedding was two months away, so I had time to think about it.

Not that I was hoping to find my happy ever after, as Tom had put it, at the wedding. That would be crazy.

Before I turned the corner to a side street, I saw Wren going into Fabulize holding a large coffee from Spilled Beans.

Wren was another guy from my childhood that hadn't exactly been straight and had come out after meeting Tom.

It seemed all around me were perfect examples of why it shouldn't be so hard for me to do this. Why did it still feel like I had such a big wall to climb?

CONNECT WITH ANA

Connect with Ana on social media:

Hang out in my FB Group:
facebook.com/groups/CafeRoMMance
Follow me on instagram: *instagram.com/anawritesmm/*
Follow me on Bookbub: *bookbub.com/authors/ana-ashley*
Sign up to my newsletter: *bit.ly/AnaAshley*

For an overview of all of Ana's books and audiobooks, visit her website: *anawritesmm.com/books*

BOOKS BY ANA ASHLEY

Single Dads of Stillwater

A spin off series from Chester Falls that can be read on its own. Each book features one or more single dads in this community of friends, family and found family. In this contemporary MM romance series you'll find heat, emotion and a guaranteed happy ever after.

Newcomer

Antagonist

Breakthrough

Heartstring

Datebook (Coming early 2024)

Finding You Series

A standalone series set across the Atlantic between New York and Portugal. Find your way home with this contemporary MM romance series with friends to lovers, star-crossed lovers and age gap with plenty of heat, feels and always a happy ever after.

Home Again

Together Again

Love Again

And for a special short story, Complete Again, plus bonus scenes, grab the Finding You boxset now.

Room for 3 series

This is a high heat MMM contemporary romance series set in an island resort.

The Resort

The Vacation (Free short story)

Chester Falls Series

From a Prince to a Happy Ever After for all, enjoy this small town MM romance series that's as sweet as they come, with plenty of heat, humor and everything in between.

How to Catch a Bookworm (Prequel short)

How to Catch a Prince

How to Catch a Rival

How to Catch a Bodyguard
How to Catch a Bachelor
How to Catch the Boss (a Christmas novella)
How to Catch a Biker
How to Catch a Vet
How to Catch a Happy Ever After
You can now have all the books in the series and the prequel all in two boxsets.
Chester Falls Collection Volume I
Chester Falls Collection Volume II

Standalone books
Christmas Bubble: a low angst, standalone, Christmas novel featuring a petite but larger-than-life cheerleader, an older demisexual football coach and a winter cabin by the lake with only one bed. With cameos from Chester Falls and Stillwater.
Midnight Ash: a sweet Cinderella fairytale retelling with a sexy kinky twist on the side, and a cast who don't quite behave as you'd expect.
Stronghold: a sweet and sexy romance in Sarina Bowen's World of True North, Vino & Veritas series. This is a standalone story between two childhood friends who reunite after as decade apart, with some creative use of maple syrup.

FREE READS
My Fake Billionaire
The Vacation

ABOUT ANA

Ana Ashley was born in Portugal but has lived in the United Kingdom for so long, even her friends sometimes doubt if she really is Portuguese.

After getting hooked on reading gay romance, Ana decided to follow her lifelong dream of becoming an author.

These days you can find her in front of her laptop bringing her stories to life, or in the kitchen perfecting her recipe for the famous Portuguese custard tarts.

Ana Ashley writes sweet and steamy gay romance set in America, often in small towns where everyone knows everyone.

You can follow Ana on the usual social media hangouts.

For access to exclusive teasers, content, and general book and food related goodness you can now join Ana in her Facebook Group, Café RoMMance - Ana's Reader Group

Ana's VIP Readers - bit.ly/AnaAshley

Facebook Page - @anawritesmm

Email - ana@anaashley.com

Instagram - @anawritesmm

Bookbub - bookbub.com/authors/ana-ashley

Goodreads - goodreads.com/ana-ashley